How I Became an AMERICAN

How I Became an AMERICAN

by **Karin Gündisch**
translated from German by James Skofield

Cricket Books
Chicago   S

First published in a slightly different form in German as
Das Paradies liegt in Amerika, copyright © 2000 Beltz Verlag,
Weinheim & Basel; Programm Beltz & Gelberg, Weinheim
Copyright © 2001 by Karin Gündisch
Printed in the United States of America
Designed by Anthony Jacobson
Second printing, 2002
Library of Congress Cataloging-in-Publication Data

Gundisch, Karin, 1948-
[Paradies liegt in Amerika. English]
How I became an American / Karin Gundisch ; translated from
German by James Skofield.
p. cm.
Summary: In 1902, ten-year-old Johann and his family, Germans
who had been living in Austria-Hungary, board a ship to immigrate
to Youngstown, Ohio, where they make a new life as Americans.
Translation of: Das Paradies liegt in Amerika.
ISBN 0-8126-4875-7 (cloth)
[1. Emigration and immigration—Fiction. 2. German
Americans—Fiction. 3. Immigrants—Fiction. 4. Youngstown
(Ohio)—Fiction. 5. Transylvania (Romania)—Fiction.
6. Romania--Fiction.]   I. Title.

PZ7.G967 Ho 2001

[Fic]—dc21

2001037223

". . . on one end of the conveyor belt, you'd place an Irishman, a Ukranian Jew, or an Italian from Apulia, and out the other—after eye inspection, inoculation and disinfection—would emerge an American."

—Georges Perec and Robert Bober,
Stories from Ellis Island

This will be a long story, because I have a lot to tell. Mama said I should write it all down, because she hasn't the strength to do it. Besides that, I'm a good storyteller. That's what Miss Miller said; she's my teacher. It's out of the question for Tata to write it, because he's working late all the time. He doesn't like the work in the steel foundry and is always dreaming that one day we can move away from Youngstown. He wants to go to California, where there are no steel mills. Perhaps we could manage a farm there. A friend of Tata's moved with his family to San Diego, which is down by the border with Mexico. We're waiting to hear from him. If things are going well for him, Tata would like us to move there as well. Before that, though, we'll once again have to save money for the long journey. Mama would rather stay here, because she's had enough of being on the road. She said I should write down everything that we lived through so that we, namely Peter, Regina, Emil, and I, could remember it all later. But I don't believe I could ever forget my journey around the globe from Europe to America. "You're deceiving yourself," Mama said. "You have a lot to experience yet, and gradually your memories will fade of the country in which you were born, of our life there, and of the great voyage."

Now that I think about it, it's because of Eliss that I have to write down our story; otherwise we'll forget her. Eliss didn't get a gravestone, because we didn't have any money. Actually, her name was Elise, but we always called her Eliss. In America, she would have been called Alice. Here, I'm called John, but it still says Johann on my birth certificate.

"Write down how you became an American," said Miss Miller.

So I begged my mother for money for a notebook, and I began to write.

". . . on one end of the conveyor belt, you'd place an Irishman, a Ukranian Jew, or an Italian from Apulia, and out the other—after eye inspection, inoculation and disinfection—would emerge an American."

—Georges Perec and Robert Bober,
Stories from Ellis Island

How I Got a Nickname

I was born in 1892, the third child of Maria and Peter Bonfert. My brother Peter was then eight years old, and my sister Regina, three. Actually, I was the sixth child, but the others died soon after birth. We didn't count them as part of us. Mama had to bear six children in order to keep three. At that point, Emil and Eliss weren't yet alive.

My birthplace was Heimburg, in Siebenbürgen, part of Austria-Hungary. Most people there work at weaving wool, and each householder owns a plot of family land or at least a garden. Our town was famous throughout Siebenbürgen for its many plum trees.

When I was two years old, my parents moved to Slatina, in Rumania, where my father took a position as foreman in a sawmill. Tata was greatly liked by the Rumanians, and some of the workers even brought us gifts of eggs and chickens. You might say we ate high on the hog in those days, and no one had to go hungry. But there were also Rumanians in Slatina who disliked the Germans, because they got the better jobs. My father explained to me the truth of this: it had to do with better education. The Germans in Siebenbürgen had always had good schools.

My father liked the work in the sawmill, but he didn't last all that long in Slatina because he was homesick for his plum orchard. One day, something happened that drove him away: he was accused of theft by a man who wanted to get the foreman's job. A whole load of oak boards had vanished without a trace from the sawmill, and my father was almost thrown in jail. He had to think quickly. Because he knew how superstitious the peasants are, he knelt down and prayed that the dear Lord would punish the wood thief forever. Out of fear of God's punishment, the real culprit then came forward, and the plot against my father was exposed. From then on, my father thought only about returning home.

In Slatina, my brother Emil was born, our fourth child to survive. My parents named him after a French engineer whom my father greatly admired. But the French *Emile* has an *e* on the end of the name, and in German that looks almost like *Emily*. So we simply left off the final *e*.

Shortly after Emil's birth, we moved back to Siebenbürgen, and into my grandparents' house. It wasn't
very large; it had only two rooms and a kitchen. My
grandparents kept the room next to the street, and we
moved into the dining room, which was by the kitchen.
Many years before, my grandfather had built a big
workshop next to the house in which there stood
two old looms. My father was actually a weaver by
trade, as was his father, and so for a while he worked
as a weaver. Although the work paid little, we had
enough to eat, because my grandmother and mother
raised a garden of potatoes, sugar beets, carrots, and
onions. They also grew field beets for the pig that we
slaughtered at Christmastime, when it had put on
some weight. When one of us needed shoes, however,
my Mother had no idea how we were going to manage.

About two years before I was born, Benjamin
Becker, a man from Bremen, came to our village. He
told the people about a better life in America.
Laborers were needed for the steel mills of Youngstown, in the state of Ohio. He told about the people
from Siebenbürgen who had moved to Youngstown,
and how well they were doing. This was news everyone was pleased to hear. When the visitor traveled
on, he left behind the address of a John Smith who
had been known as Johann Schmidt when he was
still living in Siebenbürgen. John Smith's wife Helene
was renting rooms to newcomers and doing other
things to help immigrants.

Benjamin Becker dressed up his stories with

songs that his listeners couldn't get out of their heads. Those songs made the rounds. The boys and girls, especially, liked to sing them. My sister Regina, who is very musical and who usually sings while doing the dishes, taught me the immigrant songs, because I like to sing, too. My sly sister used that to her advantage. When she had to do the dishes, she'd get me to dry them, and together we'd sing our favorite songs at the top of our lungs. One of them was "The American Song of the Rabbits," and this is how it went:

> *The world is really much too mean*
> *to us poor bunny rabbits, poor rabbits!*
> *We are begrudged a blade of green*
> *or sprout to feed our habits.*

> *For, if a rabbit dares to seize*
> *a cabbage leaf, he's shot, he's shot!*
> *And, served with salad and with peas,*
> *he's dished up from a pot.*

> *It's just a shame! I tell you so,*
> *there's nothing here to eat.*
> *America is calling, though,*
> *Let's go! on nimble feet.*

We always sang a song of praise to Columbus, as well, because he brought back news of this new world.

Our grandmother didn't like that song at all. "Anyone would think that this Columbus was the dear Lord," she'd say. "Can't you sing something else?"

Of course, we knew other songs, but even those our grandmother didn't care for:

Apples, pears, the plum, and fig;
all grow free; no need to steal.
And the fruits are just as big
as a carter's wagon wheel.

Sausages hang from the trees;
some with sixty links or more!
And the baked hams, if you please,
spring up right beside your door.

Horses are no problem, cousin,
do you wish to have a ride?
Whistle up yourself a dozen;
they'll come running, to your side.

"So you've only got to rest on your oars and watch everything growing, just like in Paradise," said Grandmother. "But don't you know that to get to Paradise you have to die first?"

But we didn't want to go to America or to Paradise; we just wanted to finish washing the dishes.

Benjamin Becker had left behind him great restlessness in the village. In the pub, or while playing cards, the men often mulled over what kind of people this John and Helene Smith could be, and whether or not you could trust them. Many folks were hoping for a better life and prosperity in Youngstown. Every so often someone would say, "If I were in Youngstown, then . . ." Yes, *then!*

Only a few weeks after the departure of the visitor from Bremen, Johann Müller disappeared from our town. When you asked his three children where their father was, they said proudly, "He is in Youngstown!"

Johann Müller never contacted his family again. He simply was gone. He never sent the travel money for his wife, and for Sami, Kathi, and Minni, and after a little while nobody asked the wife or children anymore if the father was going to send for them.

In the following years, more families left. Most of them weren't from our village; I didn't know them. The men left first, for Youngstown, Pittsburgh, or other destinations, and a few years later, they sent money to their families for the big voyage over the ocean. But there were also men who returned to their villages in Siebenbürgen and bought land and built houses with the money they had earned in America.

The father of Gretchen Schneider, who was in my class in school, wrote many letters at first. But then the letters stopped and Gretchen's mother found out from a woman living in a neighboring village that her husband had taken up with an American woman and had had a child with her. Gretchen's father didn't return, and people didn't ask after him anymore.

No wives or children from our village had made the trip yet. And so my mother was very dismayed when my father said to her one day, "Mariekins, I want to immigrate and try my luck in Youngstown, where they need workers. The weaving business is going downhill here, and I don't think it's going to get better. I don't want to wait until we have nothing to gnaw on. I see only one possible way out: immigration."

At first, my mother cried bitterly, but then she and my father began to work out plans for the future. Initially, she said nothing about their intentions to Emil, Regina, or me, because we were too small, but my oldest brother was in on the secret. Later on, my mother told me everything. She had written down many things herself in an old notebook: the day, and sometimes even the hour, when something important occurred to her. She gave the notebook to me. Mama has beautiful handwriting because her teacher in Heimburg, who was also my teacher later on, stressed beautiful handwriting.

Our parents had resolved on the following: first, my father would go to America. He would borrow the money for the trip from Grandfather. Then he would work night and day and—as soon as possible— he'd pay his debts and send the passage money for Peter. Then father and Peter would work day and night and—as soon as possible—they'd send the passage money for Mama, Regina, Emil, and me.

One morning, my father wasn't there. Emil and I went to the workshop a few times, to look for him, but only Grandfather was there. The shuttle flew back and forth; Grandfather wasn't inclined to talk and shooed us away. "Go to your mother. I'm busy!"

When our father hadn't returned even by nightfall, I asked my mother, "Mama, where's Tata?"

Mama was struggling with tears. She swallowed and cleared her throat and then she said, "Hanzi, your Tata has gone to Youngstown, and soon we'll all follow him, and there things will be much, much better for us than here."

I was then eight years old and in the second grade. Sami Müller and Gretchen Schneider were in the same class with me.

"Sami's father didn't send the passage money," I said to my mother.

Her cheeks flushed bright red. "Sami's father, Johann Müller, was a drunk," she said. "It's no wonder he went bad in America, if he ever even made it there. Perhaps he traded in his ticket in Berlin or Bremerhaven, for brandy. No, it doesn't surprise me at all that Johann Müller never wrote!"

"But Gretchen's father didn't send passage money, either," I said, after I thought about it for a bit.

"Can't you hush?" pleaded my mother. "Your father will certainly send money and in two years we'll all be in America. I know it!"

I knew it, too. My father would never leave us in the lurch. But there were some in my school who weren't so sure. When it had got around that my father was in America, fat Sepp, who was a head taller than I, said to me, "Well, when are you going to join your father?" And all the children understood that Sepp didn't believe that I'd ever get to America.

I was very unhappy that day, and didn't show myself on the street or in the neighboring garden, where we usually played cops and robbers. Instead, I passed the whole afternoon in our own garden under the nut tree. I let my thoughts wander and, in no time at all, I was with the wild Indians—the ones in the stories of those who had returned. I crept up on their campfire, and next to the sleeping Indians I recognized a paleface bound to a tree. It was Sami's father. He was being guarded only by a solitary Indian, and even that one was half asleep. I stalked around the tree (as carefully as when I stole plums) and freed Johann Müller from his bonds. He hadn't had anything to drink that day, thank God, because the Indians hadn't given him anything, and so he immediately understood that he was being rescued, as we quietly, quietly crept away and made our escape.

I was just imagining fat Sepp's face when he learned that I had brought Sami Müller's father home, when Granny called me in to supper. I had been about to rescue Gretchen's father, but I postponed that rescue, because Grandfather didn't like it when one of us came late to supper.

A few days later, Sepp pointed at me in the schoolyard and yelled, "Look at Johnny the American!"

Everyone turned and stared at me, and I ran

home and cried miserably. My brother Peter gave Sepp a thrashing at the earliest opportunity, but it didn't help much. I had gotten a nickname, and "Johnny the American" is all that the kids would call me from then on. Nobody saddled Peter with a nickname, because he was big and strong—and because nobody in the village knew how to say "Peter" in American dialect. And that's how I became an American.

We Set Out

In America, you really have to speak English well, if you want to get ahead. The Hungarians, the Slovakians, and the Rumanians hold their Sunday church services in their native languages, but in the evangelical churches of the German immigrants, there are services in two languages, because the young people soon know English better than they do German. The Germans give up their mother tongue the quickest. It's mostly because they've simply been in America for a long time, and their children have been born here. My father works with many Swedes and Irish, but also with many Germans and Austrians. Amongst themselves, the immigrants speak in their native languages, but the Swedes have to speak English with Tata, because that's the language they have in common.

Tata knows German, Hungarian, and Rumanian. Now he has to learn English, as well. But he wants me to write our story in German, so that I can practice using it. In school, I study everything in English and only on Sunday, before church services, does a teacher give us a little German lesson. In this frontier America, many languages are spoken, but English is the main language for everyone.

I don't find it hard to learn the new language, because Miss Miller pours the words into us, one after the other, the way a mother feeds milk to her child. But the language makes you laugh, until you're used to it. *Ja* is pronounced "yehss"; *Komm hier,* "kuh-mawn"; *Brot* is "brehhd"; *Fleisch* is "meeeet"; *Schnaps* is "wisskee"; *Messer,* "nife"; *Hose,* "paantz"; *Kopf* is "hehd," but that sometimes also means "hat." *Schöner Tag* is "nizedaay"; *Christtag,* "Krisss-misss"; *Neujahr,* "nooyeer." It sounds exactly like I've written it, but in English they spell it differently.

Peter, Regina, Emil, and I quickly adjusted to life in Heimburg without our father, and things didn't go too badly. Sepp and a couple others in the school made fun of Regina and me, but I learned to put up with it. If anyone asked me if my father had sent us the passage money, I answered very quietly, "No, not yet." I told them how hard my father had to work in the steel mill, how hot it was there, and how big the factories in Youngstown were. Some employed up to six thousand workers, and so much smoke hung over the town you couldn't even see the blue sky. Even Sepp was impressed that there were such big factories in Youngstown. At first, he didn't want to believe me, but when Regina confirmed it, he left me alone.

I thought about America a lot. I did my best day-dreaming sitting under the nut tree. And one day, I rescued Gretchen Schneider's father. I imagined that I found him in America, with his American woman. I convinced the American wife that her European husband had to return to his old family and—because she was already very old and would soon die—she let Gretchen's father go and gave him their newborn child and a large inheritance as well. But then Grandfather came and called me into the house and I had to go clean all the family's shoes for church on Sunday.

Three or four months after Father left, my aunt Kathi married a well-to-do man and went with him on a honeymoon to Venice. Mother didn't begrudge her sister-in-law her wealth, but from then on, she took our own poverty that much harder. She would so have liked to have that money for the journey to America!

On the day our aunt started off to Venice, we all walked to the train station to see her off. She and her husband rode in a carriage to the train, and the coachman hauled and heaved the heavy luggage into the compartment. Aunt Kathi wore a brown traveling suit from Vienna and an attractive hat, while our mother was dressed in her old Sunday dress, which she wore only on special occasions. It was a bit tight for her, and Regina had to unbutton some of the buttons on the back so that she could breathe a bit better. Nobody noticed it except Regina and me, because Mother wore a shawl that covered everything. When the train started off, we stood waving a long time, then Mother took Emil and me by the hand and we walked home. "It's about time," she said, "that your father sent for us. Little by little, I'm becoming impatient."

A month later, Aunt and Uncle returned from Venice, and they brought us each something. Regina got a cambric handkerchief with an embroidered monogram; Emil got candy; and for Peter and me there were pocketknives. We thanked them for our presents, and Mama thanked them, too. Later, she said to Peter, "What you really need is a pair of shoes. If you're going to travel to America, you at least need to have decent soles on your feet."

Regina, Emil, and I had almost forgotten that Peter was going to leave before we did. But he was thinking about it night and day, and was building a trunk out of fir, with room for all his things. He packed the chest and lifted it up to his shoulder. It couldn't be too heavy, because he would have to carry it to our train station first, and then from train to train in the stations between Heimburg and Youngstown. Emil and I watched him as he heaved the chest high. Our older brother was strong. He was seventeen years old and work had given him hands like bear paws.

One morning, Peter set out, and Mama's eyes were red with crying. Emil and I had had no inkling that our father had even sent the money for Peter's journey. At least this proved that my father was working to bring all of us to America. But hardly anyone questioned that anymore, because in the meantime, other fathers had gone across the sea. No one was much interested that my father had been the first from our village to leave his family and make the trip.

After Peter left us, Regina started acting like she knew a big secret. She was now the eldest child among us, and pretty proud of it. She began treating Emil and me as though we were small children. And I was only three years younger than she was! At first, I kept thinking that maybe she would suddenly clear off for America, too, but she was a girl, and much too young, besides, to go off on a trip all alone. Of course, there were a few young girls in our village who had emigrated without their families and had become housemaids to wealthy people in New York or Pittsburgh. In America, they no longer had to hoe potatoes or corn; they had nice clothes and a little money and they could marry when they chose. In America, nobody asked how much land or how many looms the father of the bride had before a marriage. Everyone was equal and the butcher served the customers by the order in which they came into the store, and not by their nationality. "All people are equal before

God," Peter wrote us. "Why shouldn't they then be equal at the butcher's?"

One evening in September, Mama gave birth to Eliss. She was named Elise, really, but from the start, everyone called her Eliss with a long *a* sound. Regina's long-held secret had been that Mother was expecting a child. Although Mama had seemed to be getting stouter, Emil and I had not thought anything of it. Mama had carried on with her work; she hadn't said much. Perhaps she thought that saying something would bring bad luck, because one never knew whether a child would survive birth and the first year.

When the midwife came into our room carrying Eliss in her arms, she said, "It all went well this time, too. Your sister is a strong, healthy baby."

After the birth, Mama looked very tired. Eliss was the eighth child she had borne. Now we were five siblings: Peter, Regina, me, Emil, and Eliss.

"They stand out like the pipes on an organ," Grandfather said when he saw Regina, Emil, and me at Mama's bedside. Perhaps he was counting the gaps between us.

"The Lord gives; the Lord takes away," Grandmother said, sighing. "We'll give thanks to the Lord that Mariekins has given birth to a healthy child."

We were all happy about Eliss being born. Our mother was soon jolly once again, and sometimes she even sang while doing the dishes. Eliss was our sunshine.

From America, Father and Peter wrote how happy they were about Eliss and that they hoped in a few months to be able to send us the money for our journey. Peter was now working in the steel foundry and—in contrast to Father—he liked the work. He was earning good money and he wrote American words in his letter. *"Well,"* he wrote, "it was a good decision to come to Youngstown. In old Europe, time stands still, but here, it moves forward and each day brings something new." He signed his letter Peter, but at work they called him Pete.

Tata and Peter were living with eight other men in John and Helene Smith's "boardinghouse," a rooming house, as we would call it. It was a barracks with ten beds. Helene managed the house. She made breakfast for the men, gave them a basket with food to take to work, cooked the evening meal, and looked after the washing. Every fourteen days, when it was payday in the factory, John would come around and collect the money owed for room and board.

That autumn, Mama began the preparations for the great journey. She dried slices of apple and plum and stitched together haversacks for Regina, Emil, me, and herself to carry provisions for the trip. Then she cut up sheets of linen, hemmed them, boiled them clean, and ironed them. These were the diapers for Eliss. She needed a lot of them for the trip, because on the train and on board the ship it would be difficult to wash them.

Grandfather had borrowed a map from my teacher, and in the evening, Mama, Regina, and I would pore over it, and I would trace with my finger the route of the journey. I soon knew the stations of the journey from Austria-Hungary through the German Empire and the United States of America well enough to recite them like a poem: Hermannstadt, Szolnok, Ratibor, Breslau, Berlin, Bremen, Bremerhaven, New York, Youngstown.

Then, before falling asleep, I'd repeat the wonderful names of the exotic states. They sounded like magic words, and I fantasized a whole slew of American adventures for myself. One day, I was going to break away from Youngstown and go live with the Indians and be a fur trapper. I'd send my first pelt to Mama and the second to Regina, even if she didn't deserve it. But the third, fourth, and all the other furs I'd sell. With the money, I'd buy a big piece of land and build a city on it and name it after Grandfather. Peterstown . . . or even better, Petersburg. Or Pittzburg, because all Peters in Heimburg are called Pittz. One day, Grandfather would travel over the ocean, because by then I'd have enough money to pay for his trip, and Pittzburg would suit him very well indeed.

One night, I dreamed of that wonderful town, with big houses and wide, paved streets along which streetcars and automobiles glided. In the dream, Grandfather also appeared, and I rode with him to church on a streetcar. "Something's missing," Grandfather kept saying. "I haven't milked the cow and— for the first time in fifty years—I haven't swept the street in front of the church entrance." He looked very put out.

I was quite sad when I awoke from this dream, but at the same time oddly comforted. I understand today that my grandfather never would want to come to Pittsburgh or Youngstown, but that he can milk Virak twice a day as he's always been accustomed to doing. And, on Sundays, he can tidy up the street in front of the church entrance so that it will stay clean until the evening. Grandfather is happy with his life, and wouldn't want to ride to church on a streetcar. Perhaps he is too old for American adventures.

When the passage money really did arrive, we couldn't quite believe it at first. Mama was very still and our grandparents, too, were just as quiet. Then we got used to the idea and Regina began counting the days until the departure and saying good-bye to her girlfriends. She found new ones to say good-bye to every day. She also said good-bye to Misch, who had been coming over for a while now to visit us, which Mama maintained was because of Regina. He wanted to immigrate, too, and Regina promised to write to him about the new world, and whether or not there were jobs there for roofers, because Misch was apprenticed to a master roofer. Emil and Eliss were still too small to grasp that we'd be journeying around the world. Besides that, Emil could barely remember Father and Eliss had never seen him.

I was happy about the big journey, about Youngstown, and about my father and Peter. Well, now I really *was* Johnny the American and I was going to bust loose and go to America. That was in May 1902, and I was ten years old.

From Heimburg to Bremerhaven

We left Heimburg on May 12, 1902. Mama had packed smoked bacon, dried fruit, and fresh bread in our haversacks. We had many bundles of clothing among our luggage and, of course, the diapers for Eliss. As we left our dooryard in order to go to the train, neighbors were all standing, silently, in front of their doors. We all knew we were saying good-bye forever. The women neighbors presented Mama with a bouquet of garden and wildflowers. It was the custom when someone went away. Those flowers dried up long ago, but Mama has never thrown them away. They moved with us from Front Street to Hilker Street, and lost almost all their color in the meantime, but they still smell like the hay on the meadows of Heimburg. The bouquet is now lying wrapped in paper in our linen closet. Mama doesn't want to throw it away. Regina says that we will be proper Americans only when the bouquet has turned to dust, and that will take a long time. In Siebenbürgen, we were Americans before we'd even left the country; here in Youngstown, we're only European immigrants. It's all the same to me.

Our train left Heimburg at 11:30 A.M. Aunt and Uncle brought our luggage to the station by carriage. Granny and Grandfather escorted us, and Regina's teacher and her class were waiting at the station to say good-bye to her. Regina was greatly loved by her classmates. We all knew we'd never see one another again.

From Heimburg we traveled to Hermannstadt and from there to Kopisch, where we had to change trains. We had to change many more times and we had to wait a long time at the border between Austria-Hungary and the German Empire. Nobody was interested in our passports. We had only to show our ship tickets, and then they left us alone. They simply wanted to be sure that we weren't going to remain in the German Empire.

At first, after the good-byes at the train station, we were all very sad. Only Eliss was happy; she didn't want to sit still. After we'd changed in Kopisch, Eliss fell asleep and Mama told Emil and me the story of the rat-catcher of Hamelin. I'm going to write it down here, because it's connected with the story of our family.

Some time ago, there was a man who had a job that nobody else wanted: he was a rat-catcher. Because he wore curious clothing made of patches and played the flute, he was called the Pied Piper. People turned and stared at him when he walked down the street. He could play the flute very well, and he earned his daily bread by playing it. When he played his flute, rats and mice followed him wherever he went.

One day, the rat-catcher came to Hamelin. Things were going badly with the people of that town; they had no more bread, butter, flour, or potatoes. Everything had been taken by mice and rats. The rats had even nibbled on the feet of the piglets in their sties, and the townspeople asked themselves fearfully what the rats would devour next. The mice and rats were multiplying from day to day. So the rat-catcher was a hero who came in the nick of time, for he rescued the townspeople from the plague. The rats and mice followed him down to the river, where they drowned. Naturally, the man expected to be paid by the town. But with the passing of the danger, the townspeople had become cocky, and they didn't want to give him his due. So the swindled rat-catcher took hideous revenge. On a Sunday, when all the inhabitants of the town except the children were at church, he returned to Hamelin dressed as a huntsman. He played wonderful songs on his flute, lured all of the children out into the streets, and led them into a cave in a mountain. Those children never returned to Hamelin. They did not see the light of day again until they reemerged from the mountain in Siebenbürgen.

We were descended from those children. Mama thought that the rat-catcher must have been someone like Benjamin Becker—someone who could lure people away to foreign lands. But Benjamin Becker hadn't bewitched the people by playing the flute; he had bewitched them with his stories of the wonderful life in Youngstown or Pittsburgh, and with his immigrant songs.

The story of the rat-catcher preoccupied me for a while, but the rocking motion of the train made me drowsy, and I fell asleep. When I awoke, I felt a bit sick to my stomach and couldn't eat anything. My mother and Regina felt that way too, and by the time we left the train in Bremen, we had eaten almost nothing of our trip provisions. We were dizzy and it was some time before we were once again steady on our feet.

In Bremen, we reported to the office for immigrants, where we were given some watery soup and some coffee. The food was served in dirty dishes and tasted worse than the gruel we sometimes got at home. When our mother complained, the server replied, "It's good enough for immigrants!"

There were so many people at the Bremen train station that we thought the whole German Empire must be emigrating. The people weren't only from

Germany, however, but from half of Europe. Many came from Austria-Hungary like us, or even from Russia.*

In front of the entrance to the train station, we ran into a man who threw coins at our feet, pointed at us, looked quickly about, and shouted, "Immigrants! Immigrants! Everyone come look!" Emil and I wanted to pick up the money, but Mama forbade us to do so. She scowled at the man and went on by. "After all, we aren't in the zoo," she said to us, "that we should pick up anything onlookers throw at our feet."

I couldn't tell whether anyone besides ourselves had noticed the incident, for the crush of people was great. We surely could have used the money. In front of the train station, people were hawking bread and fruit. Mama wasn't buying, because we couldn't afford to part with any of our money. We had no idea what expenses we might encounter on the long journey.

While we were sitting in the waiting room for the train to Bremerhaven, a small purse fell on the floor at Regina's feet. It was Mama's purse; she had been carrying it beneath her shawl. The tickets, the passports, and the money for the journey were in it. Eliss must have gotten her hands on it somehow, while Mama was quieting her. Almost paralyzed with terror,

---

*Translator's note: From 1867 to 1914, Austria and Hungary were united in a dual monarchy, which was allied with Germany against the threat of Russian expansion. The German Empire was a confederation of German states led by Emperor William I of Prussia.

Mama fastened the priceless purse securely around Regina's neck. Regina was now guardian of all our property. I've no idea what would have become of us without that purse.

That happened at five in the morning on May 17. Once on board the train to Bremerhaven, I soon fell asleep, since I wasn't used to getting up so early. And I had a nice dream.

Under my seat, I found a big pocketbook filled with American money. If you're honest, you have to return something you've found to the person it belongs to, so we asked many, many people in Bremerhaven if they'd lost anything. Some people we asked had lost their homes, or vineyards, and one had lost his bride, but nobody was missing a pocketbook with money. There were a terrible lot of people in the harbor and we couldn't possibly ask all of them. I thought of putting an advertisement in the paper: *Whoever lost something between Bremen and Bremerhaven should contact Johnny the American in Youngstown.*

We had no luck finding the owner of the money, so I kept it. I told myself that someone who'd just leave a pocketbook of money on the railway wouldn't miss it much, since he'd probably have plenty more at home. Now that I was truly rich, my father stopped going to work at the steel mill and began looking for a farm to buy. He was negotiating with a Californian farmer who wanted to emigrate to Europe, and it was beginning to look as though Tata would get his beautiful farm. Over and over he said to me, "Hanzi, you're a stroke of luck! You spin dreams into gold!"

No, you mean "money" I thought, because Tata's farm would cost money . . . a lot of money. He was stroking my hair gently with his big, heavy hand, and then Regina's voice was admonishing me, "Hanzi, wake up! We're in Bremerhaven."

I sat bolt upright in my seat and then, when no one was looking, I felt under my seat with my hand, but there was nothing there. Disappointed, I slung my haversack over my shoulder, took Emil by the hand, and followed the others to the railway car door. If only Regina hadn't awoken me before Tata had purchased the farm! Now I'd never know whether or not he had really gotten it, because the farmer was still hesitating over whether to sell his property or not. I was very annoyed with Regina.

At the harborside, all emigrants had to go into an enormous shed, where they were divided into three groups: men, women, and families. There we had to wait some more, until at last we could board the ship.

A sea wall had been built along the harbor, to hold back the ocean. The wall was broad and long and stretched as far as the eye could see. From it, docks were built out over the water. You couldn't imagine how many ships there were in the harbor. They came and went, back and forth all the time, like carts on the streets of Heimburg.

Our ship was named *The Great Elector* and had room for almost three thousand people. We boarded the ship over three gangplanks. In Heimburg, we knew everyone, but here, we knew not a solitary individual. Among all the people, however, there was one man we couldn't help but notice. He was standing near the gangplank over which we were boarding, and he was singing a song. The melody of that song has never let go of us. We took in the lyrics only in bits and pieces, but later we pieced them together:

> *A proud ship, bearing our German brothers*
> *sweeps on her lonely way, the ocean o'er.*
> *The white sails billow, and the pennants flutter,*
> *America is where they're headed for.*
> *They travel on the deep blue ocean's swell.*
> *Why do they leave the land that gave them birth?*
> *Because a cheating Fate their lives befell.*
> *And will America then treat them well?*
> *'Tis want that drives them from their native earth.*

We carried this song with us to America, and now, in the time that's passed, we've almost forgotten it again. "It doesn't matter," our father says. "An immigrant has to keep looking forward."

We didn't know that yet, though, as we were leaving Europe. We stood on the deck and looked back. Bremerhaven became smaller and smaller. Then, there was only blue. The sky and the ocean were one.

On Board the Ship

On board the ship, everyone was assigned a place in a berth. We were in third class, in steerage.

"It looks like the poorhouse," Mama said.

I didn't know what a poorhouse looked like. I thought our sleeping quarters looked more like a workshop without windows—one crammed to the ceiling with beds. The luggage was stacked among the beds, and anyone wanting to leave had to weave a path back and forth through people and pieces of luggage. Sometimes the food was good; sometimes, bad. There was meat at every noon meal, but it didn't smell good, so we didn't want to eat it. We were lucky that there were also potatoes every day. We still had bacon and bread from home, too.

The first time I went with Mama above deck, the wind almost bowled me over. That was May 17; many ships were underway on the ocean that day. Aboard our ship, three land birds hopped fearfully about, trying to escape a cat who was stalking them. Emil and I felt sorry for the poor birds and spent a lot of time shooing the cat away. We wanted to take the birds with us to America, but when our attention wavered for a moment, the cat nabbed one of the birds and broke its neck. Emil howled and I had to comfort him. (You had to pick Emil up and stroke him when he was crying or he wouldn't stop.)

The cat didn't eat the bird, however. It pushed the lifeless little body back and forth and then let it lie when a sailor came and chased it away.

"That's the first immigrant to fall by the wayside," said the man, and he threw the bird into the ocean. Then he noticed the two other birds. They would beat their wings helplessly and then give up, exhausted. "Their days are numbered," he said and tousled Emil's blond hair. "Hey! Immigrants don't cry!"

While we were at the noonday meal, the cat put an end to the two other birds, and from then on we called him "Birdkiller." The sailor had named him "Sparrowslayer."

During the morning of May 18, there was not another ship in sight. Here and there, a great rock stuck out from the water, and that afternoon, at four, we could see land. We were glad, even though it was only the second day of our voyage. By then, we were sailing through the ocean channel between Calais and Dover, and I asked a sailor what the lands were called. "On the right side is England; on the left, France," he said.

There were a great many ships in the English Channel, and it was at least two hours before we were through it and back out on the open ocean.

At first, the ocean is terrifying. But then, when you get accustomed to it, it can also be beautiful. Looking at it, it sometimes seems as if you're standing on a freshly plowed field.

During the voyage, we passed almost all our time in the sleeping quarters, because it was very cold outside. But sometimes I was allowed to go on deck with Emil, after I'd promised Mama to look after him and always hold him by the hand. Emil was so thin the wind could have blown him away! During the voyage, I took care of Emil for the most part, while Mama and Regina tended to Eliss. I also threw Eliss's dirty diapers over the railing into the sea. That was my job.

I had to tell Emil stories frequently, or he'd cry from boredom. I liked best the stories about Chirripik, and Emil liked them, too.

Here in America, nobody knows them. I told about Chirripik in school, and Miss Miller said I should make up more of the stories. But I didn't make them up in the first place. They really happened. That is what Grandfather told me, and since Grandfather couldn't pass them on to Emil, I had to.

One of the stories about Chirripik concerns a roasted goose, but when I started to tell it to Emil, Mama said, "Please stop that, or I'll be sick to my stomach." That was on the third day of the voyage, when everyone except Eliss and me was seasick and stayed in bed the whole time. Whenever people got up, they had the feeling they'd collapse or be sick. Still, Emil wanted me to go on with the story, because a story, once begun, is like an apple with one bite out of it: you can't just toss it away. So I told Emil the story of Chirripik and the goose in a whisper. The story goes like this:

One day, the pastor of Reichesdorf sent Dr. Sifft of Birthälm a roasted goose for his name day.* The pastor's wife wrapped it up in a sheet of white paper and then in a cloth that she tied up tightly. She placed it in Chirripik's drawstring sack. Chirripik set out down the road and walked and walked. When he was only a stone's throw from Birthälm, he sat down in the gutter on the bridge, where there was a bit of shade. He rested the sack on his knees. The goose smelled very good, and he was as hungry as a wolf. If only I could smell it a little, he thought. That can harm no one. He pulled the cloth out of the sack,

---

Translator's note: In many German-speaking countries, the feast day of the saint for whom one is named (the "name day") is celebrated just as a birthday might be. The celebration often has a religious dimension.

undid the bundle, and fumbled with the sheet of paper until he had unwrapped the goose and smelled and smelled it. And suddenly, he didn't know what came over him. "Oh, drat," he said to himself. He took out his knife from his belt, cut himself a drumstick that was peeping out of the wrappings, and he ate it, enjoying every mouthful. When he was finished, he wiped his mouth on his sleeve, tied the wrappings back up, stowed the bundle in his sack, and went on his way to the good doctor.

"From our good pastor," said Chirripik, as he presented himself.

The doctor's wife took the bundle and the doctor said to Chirripik, "Go into the kitchen and let the cook get you some brandy and a bit of bread."

No sooner had Chirripik gotten comfortable in the kitchen, however, when the good doctor ran in waving his arms about. The doctor's wife was standing in the doorway like a hen with her feathers ruffled. "You bad man, what have you done? That goose is missing a drumstick! She has only one!"

Chirripik arose from his bench very quietly. "Only one drumstick? But she only had one!"

"Don't talk nonsense," said the doctor. "Geese have two legs."

Chirripik looked through the kitchen window into the dooryard. "There, *there*," he screeched and pointed to the yearling geese who were standing about or lying on the sand. One of the ganders was standing on one leg and had hidden his other one under his wing. "You see, dear sir, even your gander has only one leg."

"Stupid idiot," cried the doctor angrily, and grabbing Chirripik by the collar, he pushed him down the steps and into the courtyard. Then he stirred up the gander by shouting, "Shoo!" The gander lowered his leg and ran away, gabbling.

"You see, you miserable idiot, that he has two legs?"

"Well, then," responded Chirripik, "why didn't the good doctor say 'Shoo' to the roasted goose?"

Most of the people in steerage were seasick during the whole crossing, and someone was always running out into the fresh air. It didn't smell very good in our sleeping quarters. It was especially bad when we got beans for our noonday meal.

To pass the time, I daydreamed. In my imaginary America, I met a rich baroness who didn't know to whom she was going to leave her castle, because she had no children. When I tried to imagine the castle, it came to me that I had never been in a castle before and had no idea what one looked like. But that didn't matter. You see, there weren't any baronesses in America anyway, and also no emperors or kings. Perhaps there weren't any castles there, either. So I turned the baroness into a rich lady who owned a steel mill and a coal mine. This lady had no children. One day, by chance, I happened to be looking for work in her steel mill, so she took me into her house, where I had to polish all the shoes. Later, I was allowed to clean her automobile, and also to drive it, and to take her on her rounds of shopping and summer vacationing. Finally, the rich lady died and left me everything. At once, I sold the steel mill and bought a big ship that stayed steady on the ocean even in the midst of storms. There were many cabins on board and the luggage was stowed away out of sight. On board my ship there was a huge hall; every Saturday night, musicians played and we danced. The passengers received good food, too: every day there were two or three desserts or puddings, and nobody ever had to throw up. Beans were forbidden aboard my ship and everyone made the journey to America happily and comfortably.

Mama roused me from my dream ship, back to reality. "Don't sleep so much," she said to me in a weak voice. "What will you do at night? Why don't you go above deck? But be careful!"

Once, while I was walking on deck by myself, I stumbled upon the kitchen. On the table, among the many things laid out for the noonday meal, I saw a pile of onions. I circled the table a couple of times until a small onion just happened to stray into my pants pocket. Then I left the kitchen hastily and made a beeline for our cabin. On my way, I began thinking of what my grandfather had once told me about a Rumanian prince who had had the right hands of thieves chopped off. But the onion was in my left pants pocket where no one could see it. Besides that, I was far away from Siebenbürgen, and that cruel prince had certainly been dead for a long time, now. My grandmother had once told me that the right hands of thieves withered quite suddenly, when they weren't even thinking about stealing anymore. Maybe that was true in the old world, but Granny couldn't know what things would be like in America. At any rate, I'd never stolen anything before, and when I gave my mother the onion, she was very happy. "My God," she said, "how happy you make me! That onion looks just like one from our garden." So we ate our bacon, bread, and onion, and it was the very best meal we had on the voyage.

The voyage lasted eleven days, instead of nine, because of the fog. When it was foggy, the ship's foghorn sounded over and over, so that other ships knew *The Great Elector* was coming. After we left the English Channel, I didn't see a single other ship during the entire crossing from Europe to America. But that could have been because we passed most of our time down in the belly of the ship.

During the voyage, Mama's milk dried up and she couldn't nurse Eliss. She got milk from the ship's kitchen and tried to accustom Eliss to drinking out of a little cup, but Eliss kept her mouth shut tightly. I wouldn't have drunk that milk either; it smelled bad. Eliss gnawed on a crust of bread and didn't want anything else. "Perhaps she's getting her teeth," said Mama. Eliss was always happy, and slept a great deal. For that reason, we didn't worry much about her at the beginning.

During the night of the nineteenth, the wind began blowing so hard that the next morning you couldn't go on deck. When I tried to go above anyway, with Emil, the wind knocked him down. The sailors were laughing and saying that that was nothing. It's true the waves weren't all that high, but the ship was rocking back and forth so much that I had the feeling I was sitting on the seesaw back in my grandparents' garden. Emil threw up; I wiped his mouth off, and threw the handkerchief over the railing.

The fourth day out, a storm blew up and then we were all seasick except Eliss. I lay in the bunk next to Emil, as sick as death. All I wanted was to be free of seasickness for just one minute, and to have plenty of fresh air. When I went above, I felt a bit better, but the constant heaving of the waves made me sick again.

It seemed to me, however, that Eliss was enjoying it. She nuzzled Mother's breast that had no more milk, pushed the cup with the ship's milk away, and put everything into her mouth she could get her hands on. "I hope she doesn't die of hunger," fretted Mama. "She's only skin and bones. If men wrote their wives about how awful this journey was, not a single woman with children would follow them."

When Mama said such things, Emil and I went above decks and walked back and forth. On one of our walks, we happened upon the singer I had liked in Bremerhaven. He was playing his guitar and singing a song that the anti-immigration people had been passing out on leaflets in the Bremen train station. Mama had taken one of the printed sheets, but had soon thrown it away. Secretly, I'd picked it up and stuck in into my jacket pocket. The man with the guitar was singing the song that had been printed on that sheet, and it went like this:

> *Buddy, stay at home, contented;*
> *earn an honest living there.*
> *Happiness won't be augmented,*
> *shouldering American care.*
> *On your hide, the sun will burn;*
> *unknown plagues, at every turn,*
> *will rain upon you day and night,*
> *and the money there is tight.*

> *Ah, how can mere words encompass*
> *my delusion and my dread!*
> *All my finely dreamed illusions*
> *wouldn't buy a crust of bread.*
> *On the journey—wretched, sorry—*
> *My dear little son expired,*
> *And my wife, made ill by worry,*
> *told me that of life, she'd tired.*

The singer didn't get any further with his song than that, because two strong young guys collared him and made as if they were going to heave him overboard, along with his guitar. They raised him way up high, but then set him back down on the deck, surprisingly gently. One of them straightened up the clothing of the frightened musician. "There, now, you're all pretty again," he said genially, and flicked a speck of dust from the man's jacket. "You shouldn't scare people with your songs, you understand?"

The singer didn't answer; he was examining his guitar for any damage. A group of gawkers had gathered and the two guys went over to them. The guy who had spoken turned to the people. "Just take a good look at him! He's being paid by the anti-immigrationists. His masters don't want all us taxpayers to move to America where it's free!" Then he grabbed the musician by the collar and hauled him up so that the musician had to stand on tiptoe and looked very pitiful. Then the guy let him go. The singer crumpled, but made sure to protect his instrument. "Sing something," the other young man commanded, "but this time, sing the *right* song!" The singer saw that everyone was watching him. He cleared his throat, hummed a bit to himself, and then, in a quiet voice, he sang a song in a language that none of the onlookers knew. He sang, squatting down on his bundle. After a while, he sang the song in German so that the two guys, but also Emil and I and many others, could understand it as well. Emil and I knew the song from home. Granny had often sung it while spinning flax. It was a beautiful song; we liked it.

A tiny, wild, little bird
perched on a willow bough

and sang throughout a winter's night
in a voice that rang so true.

O, sing me more. O, sing me more,
you tiny, wild little bird!
and I shall twine your little wings
with gold and silken threads.

O, keep your gold and keep your silk;
I'll sing no more for you.
I am a wild bird, and no one
tells me what to do.

Then the man sang the song in Dutch and in other languages that the onlookers didn't know. Lost in thought, he sat there, singing in a gentle tone, one verse after another, and before we noticed it the two loutish guys had moved on. The people listened quietly and then when it began to rain, slowly went back down below decks. The singer huddled protectively over his guitar and drew his coat over himself. Only then did Emil and I go back to Mother.

Mostly mothers with children and girls who were traveling alone were assigned to our sleeping quarters. Mama kept noticing a pale girl who was about seventeen years old. She cried a lot and was always vomiting. Mama asked her if she were seasick, or if she had some other illness. The girl didn't answer and Mama left her alone. But on the fourth day at noon, when the girl lay unmoving beneath her blanket and didn't cry any more or respond to any questions, Mama sent me to fetch the doctor. He came at once and we all had to leave the quarters. Two sailors came to carry out the girl on a stretcher. Then the sleeping quarters were thoroughly aired out, and the deck was swabbed as it was every day, and after an hour, we were permitted to return. We were glad to go back in, because it was bitterly cold outside.

That night, at the captain's request, we all went to bed early. Everyone in steerage settled down and a deathly stillness descended on the whole ship. Mama and I couldn't fall asleep, however, because Eliss wouldn't keep still. She had slept the whole day, but she was now wide awake and wanted to play with us. Then she began crying and made a mess in her diapers, and Mama had to clean her up. It stank dreadfully. Even after Eliss had quieted down, we still couldn't sleep because of the smell. "I'll go throw the diaper into the ocean," I said to Mama, and—despite our being forbidden to—I crept above deck. I climbed up the stairs in the darkness, pausing from time to time, listening to my own footsteps. It was very still on the promenade deck. The ship wasn't moving; the waves slapped quietly on her stern. The fog blurred all outlines. I threw the diaper over the railing and when I turned to go back to the stairs, four men were coming toward me, two of whom were carrying a heavy load. Ducking out of sight beside a lifeboat, hardly daring to breathe, I recognized the captain, by his uniform, and the doctor who had attended the girl in our quarters earlier that day. The captain gave the other two men quiet commands. All of a sudden, I understood what I was seeing. The sailors placed a heavy sack on a board and, when the ship's clock struck midnight, the captain said the "Our Father." Then the sailors slowly lowered the board with the body into the water. I heard the splash as it hit the water, and heard how the ropes rubbed against the railing as the sailors hauled them back up. Then the four men stood motionless a moment more with their heads bowed, before the captain murmured something and walked away. The other three followed him.

I didn't know if I'd dreamed it all or if I'd actually seen it. The fog blurred everything about me. For a while longer, I stayed, unmoving, beside the lifeboat, and I heard how the waves were slapping against the ship's hull. Then the engines started up; the ship moved on; it was all over.

Troubled, I crept back down the stairs and returned to my bed. I told my mother nothing, because I didn't want to frighten her.

The bed in our sleeping quarters stayed empty, and I was the only one who knew where the girl was. Everyone avoided looking at the empty bed; nobody put anything down on it, even though we had little enough room. Nobody sat down on that bed, and nobody asked why it remained empty.

Later, Mama told me that the girl had died from the aftermath of a miscarriage. Nobody on board the ship had even known anything about the girl's condition. She had been so terribly young, almost a child herself.

From that point on, Mama was sad all the time, and she watched over Eliss constantly. She would let me go on deck only when it was necessary, and Emil wasn't allowed to go with me at all.

Finally, in the Land of Prosperity

Cooking is easy and fast in America, and you don't have to burn wood, because people have gas ranges. Water flows into the kitchen, and it drains right back out, so you don't have to carry it from the well. Mama wants me to write this down; also, that nobody here crochets. They don't even know what it is.

Life is easier here than it was in the old country, and the food is better. My brother Peter says that's why the young women are prettier here, too. He explains it this way: if you feed a calf well, it will be pretty. Every farmer knows that. It's quite simple.

Our neighbor, Mr. Schuster, however, doesn't like America. He told me I should write down that this land ought to be called "Murderous

America,"* because not a day passes by without accidents and killings. In the steel mills, one's life isn't out of danger for a single minute, he says. All you're allowed to do is work all the time, and above all, you have to stay healthy so that you can keep working. America's a golden land for some, but not for others. Out of every thousand immigrants, nine hundred ninety-nine curse Columbus for his discovery. Mr. Schuster thinks I should send this "Murderous America" write-up to the *Agricultural News* in Heimburg as a warning to all those who want to immigrate.

It says in today's newspaper that rich Americans, like the Astors and the Goulds, have discovered the "simple life." When they take a vacation, they spend only seventy cents a day on their food; they eat no meat, drink no alcohol, and they live in tents by the riverside. They walk and sunbathe and regain their health through diet and exercise. Since my father's been working in the steel mills, I know that exercise in fresh air is healthy. Up till now, we always lived outdoors in the fresh air, but we didn't realize how healthy it was. We never took vacations. But every Sunday afternoon, when the weather allowed, we were out in the garden right through dusk, and

---

Translator's note: A play on words in the original German. The German word for North America, *Nordamerika,* sounds very similar to *Mord Amerika,* which means "murderous America" in German. Mr. Schuster is making a bitter joke.

sometimes in summer, we slept outdoors. Now that's all past and gone, but I really meant to be telling about how we arrived in America.

On the next-to-last day of the voyage, two children became ill. The women in steerage were very upset and were afraid the children had measles. If any children on board had a contagious disease, all the children on the ship would be quarantined for three weeks. Because of this, the women didn't know what they should do: whether they should alert the doctor or keep the illness a secret. In any case, measles was a contagious disease, and only the healthy were allowed into America. Maybe someone alerted the doctor, maybe not. At any rate, he came to inspect our quarters and took the two children and their mother with him. But the children merely had indigestion and a rash; by the evening, their fevers were gone.

On the eleventh day of the voyage, Tuesday, May 28, 1902, at ten o'clock in the evening, we arrived in America. We couldn't go on land yet, however. Very early Wednesday morning, at seven o'clock, an American doctor came on board and examined us carefully. We had to stand outdoors for two hours, until it was our turn in line. It was lucky we were all healthy, because it was very chilly. After the inspection, around ten, we were given breakfast, and then we could finally disembark. We were led into a huge barn built out over the water, and we had to wait there until noon. There were many American women there, selling good things to eat: bread, sausages, apples, and pastries. For fifty cents, Mama bought some bread, a Parisian sausage, five apples, and six jelly doughnuts. We ate like harvesters do after threshing, and it tasted delicious.

All of a sudden, tears filled Mama's eyes, and Regina asked her, "Why are you crying?"

"You know, for the first time, I believe that America could be the land of prosperity for us."

I didn't understand what Mama was trying to say, but I didn't ask, because Mama was smiling through her tears and looking very happy. Later on, Regina explained to me what Mama had meant. During the crossing, Mama hadn't really believed that we were on our way to a good future. But when she first felt the ground beneath her feet, when she first ate fresh bread, she was suddenly able to have faith in our American adventure. It would be a long time, though, before we could be called prosperous.

About one o'clock, all the passengers from *The Great Elector* boarded two smaller ships; they carried us in an hour to Ellis Island. After all the traveling, a few of those bound for America were sent back to Europe by the next boat. These were men and women who were ill with tuberculosis, or who suffered from a contagious eye infection. There was also a whole family who had scabies. The doctor discovered this during his inspection, because the children kept scratching at their armpits.

We left the boat at Ellis Island and at the top of a flight of fifty steps (I counted them) we were led into a room where twelve clerks were waiting for us. Here, we had to show our passports and our travel documents, and the clerk asked Mama to whom and where we were traveling, and how much money we had. The clerk wanted to see the money and Mama showed it to him. I think Mama was afraid they'd send us back because of Eliss. But the clerk didn't pay any attention to us and only wrote everything down very neatly. Then we had to surrender the tickets we had received in Bremen; they gave us American ones in exchange. By three o'clock in the afternoon, it was all over.

In the line, Mama struck up a conversation with a woman from Neppendorf. She learned from her that a woman traveling with three small children had died on *The Great Elector*. Now, here in America, they'd have to contact the husband of that woman, so that he could come fetch the children. Mama heaved a sigh as deep as the ocean, and the happiness that had seized her upon our arrival disappeared as suddenly as it had come. "The road to Paradise," she said, "leads through death. We don't even know—perhaps we're arriving in hell, instead of heaven, here in America."

The woman from Neppendorf nodded. "Everything's possible," she said, "and perhaps America's just a land like every other. I don't believe roast pigeons will fly into one's mouth here."

After changing our tickets, we had to get back on board the small ship. We couldn't get off it until eight o'clock at night. Finally we were on land again, but by the time we reached the railway, we were hungry and dead tired. Eliss hadn't had anything more to eat, and she wasn't happy any longer. Mama said that she was dehydrated, since she hadn't properly drunk anything for days, and that the cold on board ship had done her harm.

It grew dark, and Eliss began crying. That was on Wednesday, May 29, 1902.

We traveled second class. Emil and I looked out the window, but we couldn't see anything in the dark. We traveled the whole night through. When it began to grow light, we could finally see that the country-side was hilly and that there were factories all along the route, and many railway tracks. The train glided for miles past cut-down forests. "It looks to me like people here just take what they need and leave the rest lying around," said Mama, disgustedly. "The land is a mess, and everything's unfinished. But there's work in this country; there's plenty of work."

The train traveled dreadfully fast, never stopping for more than two or three minutes at the stations. There were three sets of railway tracks next to one another, and sometimes it happened that we encountered a train that was traveling on another track in the opposite direction. The train was comfortable and there was fresh water in the cars. Everything was laid out nicely, much better than on the railroad between Heimburg and Bremerhaven.

It took many hours before we got to the state of Ohio, and finally to Youngstown.

Arrival in Youngstown

It was four o'clock in the afternoon, on Thursday, May 30. Eliss had a fever and was crying. When the train pulled into the Youngstown station, Mama and Regina were terribly excited. They counted our pieces of luggage over and over, Regina tossing the bulky wicker baskets back and forth and Mama admonishing me many times to keep a sharp eye on Emil. I held him tightly by the hand, while he tried time and again to pull away. Mama carried Eliss in her arms, and the three of us dragged the luggage onto the platform. We stood, somewhat at a loss in the swirl of people, and then Mama began calling, timidly, "Peter! Peter!"

When she saw our father, the words stuck in her throat. He came walking down the length of the platform, searching carefully. His face and clothes were black with grime; he was all sweaty and looked like a beggar. I wouldn't have given him a second look, but he knew us at once and was beside himself with joy. When he bent down to Emil to hug him, Emil screamed fearfully, "No, that's not my Tata!" and disappeared, howling, behind Mother's dress. Mama was also startled by Father's appearance, but she didn't show it. Father hugged her, Regina, and me, and stroked the hand of the still-crying Eliss. Only then did Mama carefully ask him, as if it were of no importance, "Why are you so sweaty?"

"I came directly from work, and it was only because I was afraid I'd arrive too late that I didn't wash up and change my clothes. Did I frighten you with my work clothes?" he asked, embarrassed.

"Well, a little," answered Mama, relieved. "I was thinking you'd become just as godforsaken as this land."

Then Mama asked about Peter. He hadn't come to the station because he was still working. We'd see him that evening.

"By the way, do you have any money left over from the trip?" asked Father, almost as an afterthought.

"I still have twenty dollars," said Mother, uneasily.

This time, I saw my father breathe out, relieved. "I sent you everything I had, and I still had to go into debt. But that's not bad at all. I'm so happy that we're together once again."

Then he lifted our bags up high and led the way to the exit.

"I don't know how you managed to carry all this," he was saying to Mama.

She laughed. "If you only knew what I had to carry during our separation!"

All of a sudden, we were all in a good humor, and full of confidence. Emil had gotten used to the fact that the sooty, sweaty man was our father, and walked along beside him, helping to carry. Eliss had fallen asleep in Mama's arms. Regina and I were dragging the wicker crate with our bundles, and Mama was watching out that we didn't get lost in the crowds of people in the train station and on the streets.

And so we arrived at John Smith's—the first American roof over our heads. We were living in Helen's room. We couldn't expect more than that, for the time being, as Tata said. But we weren't picky, and in any case we hadn't had more than one room when we lived with our grandparents.

Helen is the youngest daughter of John and Helene Smith. We used to go to the same school. Whenever her parents rented her room to an immigrant, she had to go find a place to sleep with one of their many relatives. Sometimes she was completely confused and didn't know where she was going. She told me all this during our walks through the city. Only I knew it. Helen keeps no secrets from me.

We were alarmed about one thing: Eliss was getting worse. Early Saturday morning, Tata had to go get the doctor, who came at once, examined Eliss, and said that she had enteritis and pneumonia. He gave us a remedy for her: Mama mixed camphor with fat and smeared the salve on Eliss's belly and chest. Despite this treatment, Eliss didn't improve, and the next day she developed an ulcer under her left arm. The doctor came again and gave Mama powdered flax to make poultices for her stomach and chest. The ulcer swelled and looked as if it were going to burst. Then the doctor said that there was nothing more he could do for Eliss.

"Now only the good Lord can help us," said Mama in a tear-choked voice.

Regina, Emil, and I spent that whole day in the kitchen of John and Helene Smith, and didn't trust ourselves to go back to the room. I stood gazing out the window for a long time imagining that a miraculous doctor would come and save Eliss. And then I saw him! He was well dressed and he came walking into view from the left, carrying a bag of medicines, and disappeared off to the right. I strained to listen and see if his footsteps were nearing our door, but I could hear nothing. It had probably only been an insurance salesman or a bank clerk who had been passing by our window. I began talking silently with God, with death, and with myself: "Eliss doesn't want to go to heaven. We don't want to go to heaven, either. We'll be happy just to be able to stay together." But all the talking and pleading was in vain.

Father fetched a second doctor, who operated on Eliss. After it was over, the doctor said that Eliss had peritonitis, and couldn't be saved. Five days later, the incision began to bleed terribly, and Eliss died.

We buried her on the twenty-third of June at the Oak Hill cemetery in Youngstown. Emil cried dreadfully at the graveside, because he was afraid of the dark hole. I picked him up and promised to tell him one thousand stories, but this time it didn't help. There was no gravestone for Eliss because we hadn't the money. But even without a gravestone, we would never forget her. When I'm grown up, I'm going to be a doctor, a famous children's doctor, and then I'll make all the sick children well again, so that none of them will have to go to heaven ahead of time.

Soon after the death of Eliss, we moved to a damp, two-room apartment on Front Street. Mama spent every day weeping and asking again and again, "What did I do wrong? Why did Eliss have to die? If we'd stayed at home, Eliss would still be alive! Eliss was the price we had to pay for immigrating! The cost was too high!"

America hadn't brought us the best luck, at least not immediately. Out of eight children, only four remained to Mama, but after Eliss's death, I sometimes had the feeling that Mama no longer noticed that we others were still there. One day, however, when Emil got a bad cough, Mama awoke from her grief over Eliss, and became very fearful about Emil, who was still very thin and susceptible to illness. She was afraid that he'd develop tuberculosis. For that reason, she decided we'd have to move out of the damp apartment. As soon as Emil was better, she took us and began scouting out the city, looking for a better place to live. She especially liked the west side of Youngstown, where numerous German immigrant families had settled. We were lucky and found a place on Hilker Street. Then, after Father had settled his debts with John Smith, we moved into a larger house on Edward Street.

Regina and I went to the West Side School, where the first thing we had to do was improve our English. Some immigrants in America speak a funny mix of languages. I sounds like this: "When the *morgen* whistle blows, I take the *korb* with the lunch and *gehe* to work. After work, I go *mit* the streetcar *nach Hause,* sit *mich* down in the rocking chair and *warte auf* the paperboy to arrive."

Mama was very concerned that Regina and I keep up with our language studies. She didn't like it when we talked at the same time; she wanted us to speak nicely, one after the other.

After school, I often stood at the window, watching the people on the street. Sometimes I didn't notice a thing, because my thoughts were back in Europe, and also because I was thinking about Eliss. Her death had left us sad and silent. Mama couldn't even bring herself to write our grandparents about Eliss's death and about our unsuccessful start in America. That preyed on my mind, too, because I knew that our grandparents were waiting for news from us.

If it hadn't been for Helen, who knew all the ins and outs of the city, and who took me with her on her rambles, I might have turned into a vegetable without anyone noticing. But Helen showed me everything, and soon I knew the city better than my brother Peter, who had already lived here for over a year.

Youngstown had been founded in 1797—that's a little more than a hundred years ago—by John Young, who had bought 15,560 acres of land from the Connecticut Land Company. It was the start of settlement in the Mahoning Valley. The city is on the Mahoning River, west of the Pennsylvania Railroad. The name "Mahoning" comes from the language of the Indians, and means "at the salt marsh." The Indians and the later settlers first came because of the salt in the area. Today, there are many steel mills between Lowelville and Warren. Many immigrants from Europe came here hoping for work. The story of the city of Youngstown is also the story of those steel mills.

The trains of four railway lines all meet in Youngstown: Baltimore and Ohio, Erie-Lackawana, New York Central, and Pennsylvania. Sometimes, Helen and I stood on the Center Street bridge and watched the trains. Then the desire to travel would seize us, and we'd tell each other stories about how one day we'd run away to Mexico where the sky is always blue and the gold in the sand on the river-banks shines in the sunlight. We wanted to try our luck panning for gold. Helen told me about a great uncle of hers who had gotten rich that way, but who had drunk up his money as quickly as he had made it, and who had died as poor as a church mouse. We wanted to discover great treasure; we were agreed on that, at least. However, what we would do with our great riches, we didn't know for sure. But we could talk about it for hours, and we always reached the same conclusion: first, Helen wanted a room for herself, one that would never be rented to an immigrant; and I wanted to go with Helen as a cabin-passenger back to Europe and show her Heimburg, just as she'd shown me Youngstown.

One day, when we were standing on the railway bridge, Helen had the idea that I could sell newspapers in the train station. My English was good enough, she thought, and so, a few days later, freshly washed and combed and in my Sunday best, I went to the director of the Pennsylvania Railroad station, to enquire whether he might have a job for me. I had to write down my address and my age, and when he saw my good handwriting, he praised me for it. He issued me a license that gave me exclusive rights to sell papers in the station.

From then on, I went to school in the morning and worked in the afternoon. As a rule, I gave all the money I earned to my mother.

Immigrants from Europe arrived at the train station almost daily. I recognized them by their luggage, by their clothing, and their speech, but also by the hesitant way they looked about them for their relatives and friends. There were many immigrants living in Youngstown, and often their relatives, friends, or neighbors would follow after them. The Irish and Germans were the first to arrive; after them came the Poles, Slovakians, Slovenians, Armenians, and Russians; later, the Ukranians, the Hungarians and the Italians. Almost all of them worked in the steel mills. Maybe one day I'll be working in the steel mills, too.

Miss Miller, my teacher, says that if I keep on learning the way I have been, then I'll be able to skip a grade. I don't know if I want it, because I've made friends with Janusz Smith, who came from the Russian part of Poland, and with Martin Huber, who is an Austrian from Burgenland. We three are the oldest in the class. None of us has lived in America for very long, and we all have difficulties with the language. I don't want to be separated from Janusz and Martin, even though I'd much prefer to be in a class with kids my own age. I'm the tallest in my class, and I don't like that at all. It seems to me that all the mistakes I make in English seem extra stupid because I'm so tall. It's lucky that Miss Miller is so patient; because of her, I've been able to learn quickly. Besides that, I've got Helen to speak English with. I also practice with Regina, and Mama is learning the language from us. She's always asking us how you say or ask something in English.

Settling In

Regina was very good at school, and Miss Seeger, her teacher, pleaded with Mama to lend Regina fifty dollars so that she could undertake a course on salesmanship. But Mama was afraid of taking on new debts. She had other plans for Regina and me. Mama took a lease on a small farm at the edge of Youngstown, and with money from my brother Peter, she began building a small poultry business. Later, she was going to buy a cow, so that she could offer her customers milk and quark.* And if the business went well,

---

Translator's note: Quark is a European dairy food, mostly unknown in the United States. Quark is a bit like cottage cheese and a bit like yogurt, but not exactly the same as either one.

she would buy a horse to help with deliveries. At the beginning, though, she bought a simple hand wagon, which she pulled twice a week through the streets, peddling eggs and sometimes freshly slaughtered chickens. After school, Regina helped Mama on the farm and I went on selling newspapers.

Things changed a bit for Emil, too. Before, the two of us had been almost inseparable, but once I was in school, he mostly hung off Mama's apron strings. She pulled him through the streets on the wagon as if he were a prince.

Some Sundays, Martin and Janusz visited me on Mama's farm. The hens were laying eggs and cackling. We roamed about, talking, until we were tired and hungry. Mama brought us flapjacks she'd made at home and kept warm wrapped in a dishcloth. Janusz ate the most. I could eat ten flapjacks easily, but I never did eat that many because it would have meant that my mother had to stand over the stove all day. There were flapjacks only on Sunday, when we helped Mama on the farm. Janusz, Martin, and I gathered the eggs. Some of the hens had hidden their nests and laid their eggs there. But we usually found them. Janusz would slurp a raw egg if he got hungry, and I had to be careful that my mother didn't catch him at it. Once, she found eggshells beside a nest and said angrily, "A weasel's been up to his tricks here." I was glad she didn't ask any questions. My mother was doing everything she could to keep us from poverty; I didn't want to lie to her. So I begged Janusz to stop slurping eggs. "I'm hungry, John," he said. "I've got to eat something." He said this in such a tone that I couldn't refuse him. So I hid the egg-shells so Mama wouldn't see them.

It seemed to me that Janusz literally ate his way across the landscape during our rambles. Wild onions, apples, carrots—anything he found in his path—wound up in his mouth. His appetite must have been very great. My brothers and sisters and I had always enough to eat in Siebenbürgen and here in America, and so I couldn't really fathom Janusz's hunger.

During one of our rambles through the neighborhood, Martin caught a fire salamander. Janusz and I were amazed at his dexterity. Martin was laughing. "If a girl touches a salamander, she'll be a good seamstress," he said. "If a boy touches it, he'll be a good miner."

Janusz took the salamander and said, "Maybe I'll be a miner in a coal mine, like my uncle."

I didn't want to hold the salamander, and Martin set it carefully back down on the ground.

After Mama had leased the farm, Tata set aside for the moment his dream of moving on to California. So it was all the more astonishing when Peter let us know one day that he wanted to move on; the work in the steel mills was backbreaking. From then on, the two of us talked constantly about California and the possibility of buying land there.

"You'll be homesick for Youngstown," said my father.

"Then I'll come back," said Peter, good-naturedly. "When they've got eight-hour days and six-day work weeks at the steelworks, and when they've forbidden the twenty-four-hour shift, then I'll come back again."

"You'll work like a slave in the California deserts," said Father. "It's just as hot there as it is in the steel mills, and the work pays badly. If you play with matches, you'll wind up getting burned!"

But Peter didn't let such talk deter him. He'd seen for himself how farmers had turned into wage laborers almost overnight. Now he wanted to be a farmer again.

Peter saw that most of our fellow countrymen were handymen or day laborers in the steel mills. They swept the yards, serviced the machines, and worked as stokers in the boiler room, oiling and cleaning the machines. Some became bartenders, selling beer from a cart; others were deliverymen for big stores, or houseboys, night watchmen, carpet cleaners, or switchmen for the railroad. The women were housemaids or they worked in the textile factories on knitting machines. Of course, there were a few independent craftsmen, but when one of them had saved some money, he would become a barkeeper and open a saloon. "Hardly anybody is a farmer anymore," Peter said to Father. "There's got to be a way."

It was our mother who showed Peter the way; and it was she who was the first one willing to let

Peter go. She was afraid he'd come to grief in the steel mill. The factory bosses didn't pay a lot of attention to the safety of the workers, and the toll of injuries and accidental deaths was very high. An army of job hunters from all over Europe waited outside the gates of the factories, ready to take any spot that opened up.

Little by little, we had gotten used to the idea of Peter's leaving Youngstown. A letter arrived from Father's friend Martin Sill. A while before, he had settled in the Imperial Valley. He bought a plot of land there, cheap. This letter might have been the signal for us to pull up our stakes for a move to the West. But the news it brought was disheartening: the Imperial Valley was half desert. Day after day, the farmers would dig ditches to reach the supplies of desert water, and each night the wind would blow and fill the ditches back in. Once, Martin Sill's wife had placed a pail of fresh milk on the porch, to let it cool. When she came to fetch the milk a bit later, she discovered round holes in the rising cream. She soon found out why: nearby were several snakes who had come to quench their thirst. The little girl of the family had been playing with her doll right beside the pail. "Since then, Emma's been afraid for the children, especially the little one," wrote Father's friend.

Then, when Martin Sill couldn't work for a time after a fall from a horse, the family decided to return to Youngstown. Martin Sill didn't want to go back to the steel mill, however, and he begged Father to ask whether the Pennsylvania Railroad needed men.

Peter didn't let news like this hold him back. It was obvious to me that Peter was going to move on to America's West, where some farms on the Colorado River already had electric water pumps that were changing the land into a paradise on earth. In my heart, I had already let my brother go. I didn't worry about him, because our family had already long ago paid the admission fee to Paradise. I hoped that Peter would get to have his own farm someday, just as he wanted. I also knew, however, that he'd miss me, and I comforted myself with the thought that one day I could go and join him.

I knew that when Peter left, I wouldn't hear any more horror stories about the steel mill. Tata never spoke at home about his work in the mill, and he didn't like Peter telling those stories. I didn't especially like them either, but I wanted to know what was going on in the steel mill, because most of the people I knew were working there. My brother told me the following story:

Ion, a farmer from Rumania, became a laborer in America. One day, while he was looking for something beside the foundry hall door, he heard an ominous crack. He had the presence of mind to spring quickly out the door, and when the red-hot metal engulfed three other workers, he was merely hit between the shoulders by a glob of the molten steel.

After the accident, Ion went back to his boarding-house, where the wife of the boarding boss soothed his pain with cooled butter.

When Ion didn't appear for work the next day, the manager of the mill came in person to visit him.

"How much beer can you drink in a day?" he asked Ion, and the boarding boss translated the question into Rumanian.

"A whole case," answered Ion, proudly. He had always been poor, and so he usually drank well water and—now and then—a shot of whiskey. He'd only become a beer drinker since he'd come to America.

"Well, good," said the manager. "Every day, you'll get two cases of beer delivered to you. The steel mill will pay for the doctor and any medicines, and in return, you'll give us a written promise that you have no further claim against us."

Ion signed the statement, the beer was delivered, and a merry celebration began in the boardinghouse. The bottles were cracked open at the neck, as was usual, and the beer flowed down the throats. When Ion had had enough to drink, he instructed the boarding boss to write a letter to his wife in Rumania, since he himself could neither read nor write. He'd decided his wife should drink up the bottles of whiskey that he'd left behind when he'd gone voyaging. He was having a great time, and he wanted her to have one, too.

The happy drinking bout lasted until an older laborer came to look in on Ion and explained to him that the management had deceived him. He shouldn't have signed anything; there were actual laws for the protection of workers. But Ion had waived them all for a couple cases of beer. Ion's pleasure in the beer evaporated. He didn't even want to see the bottles anymore, and all of a sudden, he was stone-cold sober.

From that point on, Ion told anyone who cared to listen why he no longer liked beer.

Workers who had been laboring in the steel mills for a while were always demanding better conditions and more safety in the workplace. Peter, along with other steelworkers, had begun explaining to newly arrived immigrant laborers about the dangers in the steel mill and making them acquainted with their rights, so that they didn't wind up like Ion.

"Actually, to get better working conditions, you have to strike," my brother said.

Mama responded that Peter had become an anarchist and a revolutionary, and she knew those people led dangerous lives. At Ellis Island, she'd even been asked if she were an anarchist or a revolutionary. She'd said no with a clear conscience, and they had to let her in. Mama was worried about Peter. She was fearful about the next strike and so was willing to let Peter move west. It seemed to her that he'd be in safer territory there.

Every second Sunday, Peter had the day off, after having worked a twenty-four hour shift. Then, the two of us would find a shady spot on Mama's farm and dream about California.

"Now's the time to buy land there," my brother said on one of those Sundays. "Right now, land is cheap. When they've established electric irrigation plants all over, the prices will go sky-high."

But Peter had too little money saved to buy land, and so we would argue about how to earn a lot of money quickly. We agreed that we needed an invention—a patent on something that everyone would need. It was a shame the telephone had already been invented! The first one in Youngstown had been installed over fourteen years ago. Unfortunately, the automobile had already been invented, too. At least fifteen automobiles drove on the streets of Youngstown. My brother felt that all the necessary things in the city had already been invented, but that there were greater possibilities in the country.

So, one day, I invented the eggmobile for Mama. She always transported her eggs very carefully, but we still wound up eating scrambled eggs all the time. I began thinking that her wagon could be improved. Instead of iron hoops on the wheels, it should have rubber tires, like an automobile. Mama only smiled over my proposal, and Peter said that you couldn't get rich with an eggmobile. I'd have to come up with something really earthshaking, like the electric light bulb, for instance. But even that had already been invented, and Thomas Edison, the inventor, came from not very far away. He was from Milan, Ohio.

A Real American

Together with Janusz, I skipped a grade. One day, Miss Maier, my new teacher, asked me whether I'd gotten accustomed to America. "I don't know," I answered. To tell the truth, I really didn't know whether I'd become a proper American yet.

Janusz told me his father had changed the family name, so that they'd become Americans faster. When he had been asked by the clerk of the immigration commission on Ellis Island what his name was, he had given their Polish name, Kowalski. But the Irish clerk didn't understand Polish so he asked the interpreter what the name meant. "Smith," said the translator. "Smith?" enquired the clerk and Janusz's father had nodded approvingly.

Our name can't be made American. Bonfert comes from *bon fer.** Mama says our ancestors were iron-workers from Lothringen, who moved to Siebenbürgen many hundreds of years ago. We're going to keep our name. You see, I think you can be named Bonfert *and* be an American.

One thing is clear to me: in America, we changed from being stationary weavers and farmers to being wandering gypsies. We never stayed long at any place, and we were always moving to better apartments and houses.

We had moved, yet once again. My parents had saved every cent they could spare, and bought a small house on Dennick Avenue. The neighborhood was rural, and the streets weren't paved, so Mama could keep the cow, the pig she was fattening up for Christmas, the chickens, our dog, and the cats.

Shortly after the move, Tata began building a barn, and Peter helped him with it. He put off his departure to early the next year.

The first time Helen visited us in the new house she couldn't get over her astonishment. "You've done so much in such a short time," she said. She stayed over with us once in a while. Then I shared a bed with Emil and she slept in mine. Sometimes she came to the train station with Janusz, while I was selling papers. Janusz looked a long time for work, but couldn't find any at first. Then he left us to go

---

* "Good iron."

work in a mine. He was thirteen years old and his parents had given a sworn affidavit that he was already fourteen. In Pennsylvania, it's illegal for children under the age of fourteen to work in the mines. But Janusz had to earn money. He's the second-oldest of eight brothers and sisters. His father is a day laborer; his mother makes artificial flowers at home, and the smaller children help her. What they all earn doesn't stretch far enough, and that's why Janusz had to leave school early, although he was a good student and was eager to learn. An uncle got him a spot as a breaker boy. Now he sits on a bench, ten hours day, bending over coal that's passing by on a conveyor belt. He breaks it up and sorts out the good ore from the useless rock. Next to him sit other boys who are doing the same thing.

Our teacher was sad that Janusz had to leave school. But in our class, we're pretty much used to immigrant children simply dropping out. Sometimes it's because they've got to work, or because their parents have moved on in search of work.

When I told my older brother that Janusz had become a miner, he paced the room angrily, then stopped in front of me and said, "Almost three hundred thousand children under fourteen are working in factories, in mines, in the slaughterhouses in Chicago, or in the cotton fields of the South. They're working ten hours a day for starvation wages. Do you know what the kids from the textile mills in Philadelphia were demanding on their placards during the last strike? *We want to go to school!* Child labor should be forbidden!"

Peter looked hard at me. "Johnny, promise me that you'll succeed in finishing school, and that you'll learn something, because that's your best chance!"

I promised him.

A day later, the telegraph operator on the Pennsylvania Line asked me whether I'd like to apprentice with him when I finish school. He told me that the Italian engineer Guglielmo Marconi had invented a system that would allow wireless transmission of news across the Atlantic. Telegraphy had a great future. This sounded exciting, but what really convinced me was Mr. Baker himself. His railwayman uniform was splendid and he looked like he had the world on a string. So I decided to become a telegraph operator. It wasn't an easy decision to make, because, since I'd been selling newspapers, I'd been reading them, too. It had occurred to me that one day I could write those news articles myself.

Last summer, Regina finished school. She took an apprentice position as a housekeeper with a prosperous German family who have been living in America for a long time already. She usually came to visit us when she had time off. She couldn't help Mama on the farm anymore, but in the interim, Emil had grown up a lot and had become Mama's assistant in egg-gathering and selling.

Meanwhile, Peter emptied and cleaned out the old fir chest with which he'd immigrated. He brought it up to our room. Mama had been storing the corn for the hens in it. The chest reminded us that Peter was to be the next one to leave the family.

At Christmastime our parents decided to have a big celebration, since the year had been a good one for us. It's true the house wasn't paid for yet, but the burden was bearable. Mama was making a good income with eggs, chickens, quark, and fresh milk; Peter and Regina were earning their own money, and even I had my small earnings. Tata, of course, was our principal breadwinner, but we all contributed to our well-being, as far as we were able to.

Shortly before Christmas, we slaughtered a pig. Regina fled to the attic and covered her ears. She'd become very sensitive since starting to live with the well-to-do family. But she still liked sausage. Tata asked a Siebenbürgen man, a butcher working in the steel mill, to slaughter the pig. Mr. Herbert came willingly. He knew all the old recipes for boiled, roasted, and molded sausage. He spiced the meat just the way our grandfather used to, and he even knew someone who had built a smokehouse in his backyard and who would smoke sausages and hams for a few cents.

Mama set aside a portion of the fresh bacon so that we'd have enough for rashers and lard. It smelled like Siebenbürgen in our house on Dennick Avenue and we were very happy.

On Christmas Eve, we made a celebratory dinner like the ones we used to have: broiled sausage with sauerkraut and cornmeal mush, and for dessert stewed prunes. I ate like a starving man, and not even Regina could resist eating her fill. It all tasted so delicious to us.

After dinner, Mama did the washing up and Tata drank another glass of wine. Regina and Peter disappeared into the living room, while Emil and I had to stay in the kitchen. Something top secret was going on in the living room. I had some idea what was taking place, but when we were all called to come in, I was still very surprised. In the middle of the room stood a real Christmas tree with lit candles, just like we'd had at Christmas at my grandparents'. For an instant, I had the feeling that I was in another land and in another time, but when I turned to look for Granny and Grampa, the door opened and an American Santa Claus came in. Everybody except Emil knew immediately who it was. He spoke English with a Siebenbürgen accent and was the spitting image of Peter. When Emil finally recognized who the Christmas visitor was, he made such a fuss that Santa Claus had to flee into the kitchen and change himself back into our brother. Everyone laughed, and for the rest of the evening, we were all in high spirits.

Around eleven, my father got out his old violin, which had emigrated with him and which he hadn't played for a long time. He tuned it. We sat as still as church mice and waited for the music. The rough hands of my father, which had worked in the steel mill and had built a barn, drew wonderful sounds from the violin: *O, Tannenbaum* and *Silent Night,* songs we had almost forgotten that we knew.

At midnight, there was cake and tea. Mama had made cookies, marbled cake, stollen, and Linzer pastries, and the whole house smelled of vanilla and cinnamon. We laced the tea with rum. The bottle of rum was passed from hand to hand. Emil and I measured the rum very carefully into the small spoons, but Tata and Peter let it overflow their spoons and spill generously into their tea. Mama and Regina took only half a spoon each, and Regina made so much fuss over it you'd have thought she never had anything but milk in her tea for her whole life. Later, Mama brought out a basket of nuts. We ate and talked. Regina told us about her family, of the two children, Jenny and Carl, whom she almost missed a bit, even on this evening, and of her future plans. She wanted to be a teacher. Mama was astonished by her plans. "Don't you ever want to get married and have children?" she asked Regina.

"Oh, Mama," my sister answered, "the times are changing. By the time I want to have children, teachers will certainly be able to get married."

But when Peter started talking about his upcoming journey to California, Mama became sad. Tata tried to comfort her. "Mariekins, maybe we'll follow him later!"

"And the house?" asked Mama.

"We'll sell it!" Tata was talking as though it were a matter of eggs and milk. We looked at him in wonder.

"A man from Siebenbürgen," said Mama, "would sell his house and his homestead only in direst need. It seems to me that you've become an American!"

We kept talking for a long time, until Mama noticed that Emil had fallen asleep on his stool, with the cat in his lap. My eyes were closing, too.

Early in the new year, Peter started out for California, with his chest made out of fir, which now had a handle made of wire and wood and was a lot easier to manage. Before he went, Mama insisted that we have a photograph of the family taken. So, one Saturday morning, freshly bathed, combed, and wearing our best, we went to Mr. Brown. He was a well-known photographer, whose store I'd often marveled at. He took wedding pictures, family pictures, and portraits. He'd put some of those pictures in the display window of his store so everyone could gawk at them.

Mr. Brown asked Mama and Tata to take seats on a sofa. Regina was to stand by Tata, Peter behind him, I beside Mama, and Emil on a footstool at Mama's feet. The photographer pointed a strong light at us and observed us through his apparatus. He tugged at Tata's tie, placed Mama's hand on top of Tata's, pushed Emil more into the middle, and asked Regina to smile. Then he looked through the apparatus again, but he was still not happy with us. Peter was standing too straight, and I was too slouched over. Peter put his hand casually into his pants pocket and I straightened up. Then the photographer arranged us a whole different way: I was to sit next to Mama, Regina next to Tata, Emil on the footstool, and Peter standing behind our parents.

This back-and-forth all went on for some time, until the photographer lost his patience and finally snapped the picture. When everything was over and done, Mama was feeling poorly. Regina loosened the back of her dress and the photographer brought her a glass of water. Mama took a swallow and Regina laid her jacket over her shoulders. Then Mama breathed deeply. I looked inquiringly at Regina and she nodded her head, yes. However, when we were back out on the street, I still wanted to make sure.

"Is Mama going to have a baby?" I asked in a whisper.

"Yes," Regina whispered back.

On April 27, 1904, shortly after Peter had departed for California, my brother George entered the world. He was fifty centimeters long and weighed three kilos.

George is the first native American in our family.

It seems to me that I've been writing down my notes for him, as well, so that one day he'll come to learn how we immigrated and how we became Americans.

Maybe We'll Get Rich

Good Lord, did we have a lot of guests at Dennick Avenue! Our house was small, and the guests slept anywhere they could find a free spot. Since we'd been in Youngstown, many people from Heimburg and the surrounding area had come, because any immigrant could find work here immediately, and that was the most important thing at the start.

Our sheets had gotten very thin from being washed all the time. Once, when Mama was hanging up washing yet again, she said, "I'd be happy if the Heimburgers went to a boarding-house; that's what they're there for. Sometimes our own house seems like a stranger's to me. The guests come and go, and all I do is wash and clean and cook."

"Don't complain, Mariekins," Father said. "We're a lot better off than those who are just now arriving from Europe."

Mother wasn't complaining, but the work on the farm and at home was too much for her; even more so now that she needed her strength and time for George, who cried a lot at night and who always had messy diapers. She stood at the washboard almost every day, washing diapers, my father's work clothes, or bed linens. When the rest of us were small, our grandparents had looked after us, but now there was no one except Emil and me who could help Mama. So Emil and I decided that we'd raise George together. Helen gave us good advice and also got an old baby carriage for us. On Sundays, when the weather was nice, the three of us made off with George and took turns pushing the baby carriage around town, while Mama and Tata attended to their chores or slept in. Mama often said, "What good children we have," and Tata nodded in agreement.

One day, Helen brought her father for a visit. Mama had cleaned the house from top to bottom and Emil and I had scoured the steps so that John Smith would see how well we were doing in America and how shipshape everything was at home. John Smith wasn't at all interested in our house, however, nor in Mama's farm.

"Those hens'll eat you out of house and home," he was saying. "At this rate, you'll never make a go of it. You've got to tackle things differently."

"How, differently?" asked Tata, completely perplexed.

"Well, for example . . ." said John Smith and then offered himself as the example. "Why don't you open a boardinghouse?"

We all went into the barn, Helen carrying George in her arms, and John Smith paced out the dimensions of the building. He hemmed and hawed and then said, "If you want to convert your barn into a boardinghouse, I'll help you. I can give you a loan on the same terms as the bank. If you want, you can begin the reconstruction tomorrow."

How proud Tata and Peter had been about building the barn! They'd hardly had time to use it, and now they were supposed to give it up. It all was moving too fast for Tata.

"I think Mr. Smith is right even if I was enjoying my chicken farm," said Mama, sighing. "Little by little, I'm beginning to understand that we've been thinking too much like Europeans. I wanted to transplant our old life to America, but even I can see that things move much faster here and that we have to adjust to new circumstances. And the truth is, we're *already* keeping a boardinghouse; we're just not earning anything from it." Mama was writing off her chicken business before John Smith's idea was even a day old, and before Tata had even come to a decision.

So it came about that Mama reduced the size of her chicken flock, and Tata began renovating the barn. He missed my older brother, who was much handier than I and who had hands like bear paws and a strong grip. My hands, by contrast, were small, and I got blisters on my palms from construction work. "Never mind," Tata said, "someone's got to be a telegraph operator. Not everyone can be a farmer, a steelworker or construction worker." Or a nursemaid, I thought, and left George to the care of Emil, who had a lot more time than I. I had to go to school, sell papers, and help Father. Still, sometimes I had to mind George. Mama and Emil had work to do on the farm, and then I'd stay home, to do my homework and keep an eye on George.

Once, when I finished my work very quickly and saw how peacefully George was sleeping, I decided to take a walk to look at the automobiles on the city streets. I was going to come right back, but when I saw Mr. Henry Mayer's big car, which seated six people and had cost twenty-thousand dollars, I forgot all my good intentions and stood goggling at that technical marvel so long that George woke up and squalled loudly enough for the neighbor woman to go get Mama from the farm. But I didn't know all that then, while I was standing marveling at Mr. Mayer's car. I was imagining that one day I'd own one myself, a red one with black leather seats: one so big that it would seat all of us. We'd drive to California in that car and visit my brother on his farm. Of course, when she saw the first automobile in Youngstown, Mama had said she'd never get into one because they drove so terribly fast. A fast automobile could do thirty-six miles in thirty-five minutes. That was really too fast for Mama, as well as being too dangerous. I wasn't afraid of driving, however, and my greatest concern was that it would still be a very long time before I'd have the pleasure of trying it out. Car owners were all very rich; we were poor compared to them. But maybe we'd get rich, too, someday. You never could tell.

When I stood at a street corner, keeping my eyes peeled for cars, I always hoped that one day one would come by whose owners would let me pay to take it out for a spin. I wouldn't mind paying for that luxury, even if it cost me my whole week's income. But no such automobile ever came by. Perhaps those autos existed elsewhere, but not near us. John Smith seemed rich enough to me to buy an auto and then rent it out. When I proposed this business to him, he smiled and said, "It's a nice idea. But not for me, I'm afraid. My day hasn't more than twenty-four hours in it, and every one of those hours keeps me busy. Maybe you should be a mechanic, if you're interested in cars. Or an engineer; you've got a good head!"

Sure, there were many great things in my future; for the present moment, however, I didn't know how I was going to dare go home. It had begun growing dark, and I began thinking that George must have woken up long ago and been hungry, and there I was on the street, far away from home.

I went quickly, running the last bit. When I got there, I first crept around the outside of the house.

Mama had lit the lamp, and was at the stove. Emil had gone to sleep, his head on the table next to the Bible; I couldn't see George. Perhaps he was lying on my parents' bed. It was quiet in the house; I could hear no noise outside. I stood for a while, and looked through the window, as Mama plucked a chicken. The hot water with which she had scalded it was still steaming in the pan. The feathers were coming out easily and Mama was singeing the down off over the stove's open flame.

I was glad I didn't have to kill the chicken. I certainly knew how to do it, but I didn't do it happily. You had to put the chicken on a chopping block and slit its throat through with a sharp knife. You had to do it quickly, so that the chicken didn't suffer needlessly. The hen's body would then flap about a bit, here and there, if you didn't hold onto it. When I killed the chicken, I didn't have much appetite afterward for dinner. Tata says there are slaughterhouses for cattle and pigs and maybe also for chickens. I'd rather not imagine what goes on there.

I saw how Mama was washing the chicken, drying it off, and wrapping it in a clean dishcloth. It had to be for her customers. Perhaps she'd soon be leaving the house to deliver the fresh chicken this very evening to the cook of some rich house. It looked to me like Mama was preoccupied; maybe she was worrying about me because I'd run away, or it might only be that she was tired. I went into the house and prepared myself for Mama to scold me or to box my ears. But

Mama only looked very sadly at me and said, "I can't rely on you, Johnny. You'd rather play than help me, but you should know that I'm at the end of my strength."

I was very sorry about my mother and I was ashamed that I wasn't reliable. I promised her that in the future it wouldn't even cross my mind to leave George alone when he was in my care. Mama listened to me, and then said, quietly, "Maybe I expect too much from a child." But she didn't expect too much of me, because from then on, I paid careful attention to my little brother; sometimes I took him with me in the baby carriage to look at cars— although he wasn't much interested in them, because he was really too small.

Regina Sneaks Out

The family employing Regina moved to California, because Jenny and Carl's father had found good work there. He was an insurance agent, and California would be a gold mine for him, said my sister. He'd really get rich there.

"Maybe he'll buy an automobile, then," I said to her. *"First,"* began Regina in a tone which showed me she thought I was an idiot.

"Fifth," I said, just to annoy her. She looked at me scornfully. "What do you know about being rich, anyway? The really rich have a piano shipped in from New York, and get a telephone."

Of course, once again, Regina was right. I didn't know any truly rich people.

The wealth of some people, however, could make life for some others fairly uncomfortable.

I'll give you an example. When Carl and Jenny's family left for California to become rich, Regina moved back home again, until she could find a new position. My father shoved another bed between Emil's and mine, and now it was as crowded as it had been in steerage. We now had a single bed, and it was as big as the whole room. Or, maybe the whole room was as small as our bed.

Emil had been working for a while at a bakery; mornings, before he went to school, he delivered rolls. The baker paid him with bread and a few cents. Since Emil had gone into business, Mama didn't have to bake bread herself anymore. Until then, she had always baked bread once a week whenever it was possible—two great big loaves and several smaller ones, one for each of us. The best thing about her bread had been the fresh crust. "In America, they mill the flour too fine; that's why the bread isn't like it was at home," Mama said. But the American bread tasted good to us just the same. Emil couldn't remember what the earlier bread had tasted like; even I could barely remember it. Mama had always had to get up very early to bake fresh bread for Tata's lunch basket before he went to work. Kneading the dough had been very taxing, she said. I think she was happy that Emil was being paid in bread. The bakers' parents came from Germany and talked German to him; sometimes they made him a present of day-old cake. The baker and his wife were friendly to Emil, too, when they had the time. Most of the time, though, they didn't have any time. They were always loading the hand cart and saying, *Hurry up!*

Our brother Peter liked all bread. He said that you just had to be hungry and have money, and then it didn't matter who baked it. Only Regina insisted that the bread, and, for that matter, all the food at Jenny and Carl's, had been much better and that it couldn't be compared to what was served at our table.

Regina talked all the time about her lost family. Sometimes, she cried in secret underneath the bed-covers, because she didn't know what was going to become of her. There were plenty of openings for housemaids, but Regina wanted one with a family who would be at least as good and as refined as her California family.

When I brought the newspaper home, Mama looked for a position for her. There were always advertise-ments for positions, even in the German-language newspaper, but Regina didn't want to apply for them. Mama and Tata didn't know what they were going to do with her.

One Saturday evening, Regina took me along to meet a friend of hers who was working as a house-maid for a family who were friends with Regina's California family. She had wanted to go alone, but our parents felt it would be better if I went along, too. It would have been best, of course, if Peter had been able to escort her. But he was in California, so it was left up to me to guard Regina.

My sister, however, didn't want to be guarded. We'd hardly gotten to the next street corner when she was saying to me, "Look here, John! I'm going to meet Hilde and the two of us are going dancing, and you should go to see Helen, or better yet, Martin, and spend the evening with him. At ten o'clock, come on by the dance hall and we'll go home together."

I followed her toward the dance hall, not daring to contradict her. But when we turned the next corner, I had to ask, "Why did you make up a story to tell our parents?"

"Because their heads are still in Europe; only their feet made it to America," she said.

I didn't understand. Our parents were old-fashioned, Regina explained, and couldn't understand that young people wanted to lead their lives differently, and that there wasn't anything wrong with that. In our native land, mothers and sometimes even fathers went along to dances and kept an eye on their daughters. The old ladies sat on benches around the room and the young people danced in the middle. In America, things were different. Young people had a lot more freedom. They went to dances without their parents, danced new dances, and drank brandy. Newly immigrated parents just couldn't understand. Mama and Tata would never allow Regina to go to a dance alone. They didn't know the young men and their families, and they were afraid that Regina might take up with bad company, or fall in love with a Catholic or a young Orthodox man or even with an Indian. That just went to show once again how different everything was in America, Regina said. Personally, I didn't know many Catholics or Orthodox people, and also, unfortunately, no Indians. But I didn't think Regina knew many, either.

Hilde was waiting when we reached the hall where the Irish danced. Regina and Hilde didn't dare go to the German one, since our parents might find out about it. We peeked through the window, but the two girls still hesitated to go in. We were standing about, when a young man came and spoke to the girls in English. They giggled like silly geese, whispering to one another, and the young man laughed and invited them into the dance. But Regina and Hilde lost their nerve and my sister said, "C'mon!" to me and headed off toward the German dance hall. But even there, the girls didn't immediately go in. First we stood beside a shed, while Hilde took a wooden match out of her handbag, burned it, and used it to darken my sister's eyebrows. Afterward, Regina did the same thing to Hilde. It looked very funny, and I really wanted to burst out laughing, but I was afraid that Regina and Hilde would think I was an idiot. "Are you prettier now?" I asked cautiously.

They giggled and nodded. Then they chewed on peppermint leaves to sweeten their breath and rubbed their lips with a lipstick that was almost certainly made out of dog fat. Mama is always saying that lipstick is made out of dog fat and is bad for your health. Some women still use it in order to attract men, thinking that it makes them prettier. But I can't imagine that guys would want to kiss lips with dog fat on them, and so I thought that meant Regina and Hilde must want to discourage the boys. And *that* made me stop to think about whether Mama may not have gotten it wrong.

The dance hall had high windows and you couldn't see in from the backyard. However, the girls wanted to know who was in the hall; maybe some mothers had shown up. So they made me climb a ladder up onto a shed and look into the room from there.

"You see anybody you know?" Regina asked.

I saw almost nothing, because the windowpanes weren't very clean. Besides that, the room was so crammed with people that I couldn't make out one from another. So I said I couldn't see any familiar faces, and then they let me climb back down.

We went up to the entrance of the dance hall and Regina impressed on me that I had to be back by the shed at ten o'clock. Then the two girls left me and I was alone. I didn't know how I was going to kill all that time. I didn't want to go to Martin's because on Saturday nights all the Austrian relations came to his house to visit. His parents and his aunts and uncles would all be asking me about my family, and I couldn't tell them where Regina was just then, because all those people were newly immigrated and wouldn't understand.

I decided to wait nearby the dance hall, and

because the time was dragging by, I climbed back up the ladder and onto the shed. I wish I could have seen Regina or Hilde! With my sleeve, I rubbed a spot clean on the window; it seemed that I did recognize a few faces. I was listening to the music, first a waltz, *Wiener Blut, Wiener Blut,* then something American, something newfangled, and the couples were dancing like crazy. They didn't even pause, but kept dancing and dancing until I got dizzy watching them.

Suddenly, the ladder fell down, and I heard a woman's voice cry out. A man's low voice quieted her. "There's nobody here. We just knocked over a ladder."

"Come on, we'd better go back into the hall," whispered the woman's voice, anxiously.

"But I still want to kiss you," the man was saying.

Dog fat, I thought. He can't see it in the dark! I held myself very still because I didn't want them to find me. What they were doing exactly, I didn't know. They were breathing heavily, at any rate, and at the end, the girl said, "If my father only knew!"

If my parents only knew, I thought, that I'm sitting in darkness on top of a shed, the prisoner, in a manner of speaking, of two forbidden lovers, while in the dance hall Regina and Hilde are enticing men with dog fat on their lips and blackened eyebrows! I would be silent as the grave about this evening; I only wished that Regina and Hilde would hurry up and come out and that we could go home. Then I'd only have to lie a little bit about how nice the walk had been, and then I could creep under the covers. How I longed for my warm bed! Emil had probably been asleep for ages!

In the meantime, the windows had been covered from the inside, and so I couldn't see anything more. I decided to climb down from the shed, just as soon as the lovers had cleared off, and go fetch my sister from the dance hall. After a time, the couple went back into the hall and I was dismayed to find that I couldn't get down from the shed, because the darn lovers had tipped over the ladder and hadn't stood it back up again. Now I was really stuck, and Regina would be looking for me until dawn. I blubbered and shivered and promised myself I'd tell everything if only I could get back down off that filthy shed. I was wearing my Sunday clothes, and I had certainly ruined them. The sleeve of my shirt had greasy soot stains. It even smelled of soot. At home, at my grand-parents', it smelled of hay, of rain, of potatoes baking, or of snow, and sometimes even of manure or cow and pig dung. Here in Youngstown, it always smelled of coal and of soot.

I was very unhappy and the time passed very slowly. I had no idea how late it was. Here, you couldn't even tell the time by the moon, because the sky was always clouded over. The way things looked, I'd have to spend the entire night on the shed. And all because my sister wanted to go dancing without my parents knowing about it!

After a long time, I once again heard quiet voices. Another pair of lovers, I thought, and wondered whether I should ask them to stand the ladder back up.

"Where's the damn rascal, anyway?" a female voice was saying. It could have been Hilde's. The second voice whispered back, "He has no way of knowing how late it is."

I called, "Here I am!" and the two were so startled that there was dead silence and I thought for a moment that I had been mistaken. But then I recognized Regina's voice asking cautiously, "Johnny, where are you?"

"Up on the shed," I answered, just as cautiously.

"Oh, you poor thing," said Regina. She found the ladder and leaned it up against the shed, and I climbed down.

We went home peacefully. Hilde and Regina cleaned their eyebrows and lips with their handkerchiefs before they parted.

"Swear to me," said Regina to me, "that you won't say anything at home."

I promised to keep silent. At the same time, I decided that I'd write this story I couldn't tell anyone in my notebook. I've started keeping my notebook under my mattress, so it doesn't fall into anyone's hands. From now on, I'll write down all my secrets in it.

Time is Money

Youngstown lies on the watershed between Lake Erie and the Ohio River. The region features ridges of hills that rise up to 858 feet high. The soil is good and the earth is rich in minerals. We learned all this in school, and you can see the hills from the outskirts of town. I've gotten so accustomed to Youngstown that I can't remember what it looked like in my old home. I keep thinking it looked something similar. Mama says that's not true. Where we came from, there are high mountains, the Carpathians, and there are no big cities. The villages are small, and most people live in the country.

Recently, my parents have been talking less and less about Siebenbürgen. Before that, though, my father was always comparing everything with his old homeland. "It was different at home," he'd say, and that might mean that it was better or it was worse, but it was different. Now he rarely compares. I think he's gotten used to America. Mama, however, still sometimes finds it hard.

A few days ago, when I came home from school, I could already smell from the street that Mama was making soap, even though soap is cheap in America and everyone can afford to buy it.

I said to Mama, "Why are you always making soap? It stinks so badly. You know you can buy it."

"But what will I do, then, with the rancid bacon, the old grease, the pork rinds? You know we always made soap at home every summer."

"You could just throw all that stuff away," I said. But Mama can't throw anything away. She hems handkerchiefs out of our old shirts, and makes my old pants into new ones for Emil. She makes diapers for George out of old bedsheets. She can't even throw a pot with a hole in it away. You can keep old bread in it, and then make breadcrumbs out of that.

"At home, at my house," Mama was saying, "every year in the summer, Aunt Louisa would come to make soap. We'd make a fire in the dooryard, and put a big copper kettle on top of the tripod. Once, she made a whole pig into soap. It had the red murrain, a pig disease."

"And was the soap red?" I asked.

"Oh, no it looked just like all the other soap."

As luck had it, I didn't have to help Mama making soap. Mama placed the big kettle on the stove, poured in water, added lye and the leftover fatty parts of the pig, and stirred it from time to time. After three or four hours, the soap was cooked. Mama scooped samples out with a spoon, let them cool and tested to see if the soap was firm enough. Then she took the pot off the stove. The soap was swimming in the lye in yellow-green pieces. Mama let them cool and the next day she scooped the clots of soap out onto a drainboard and chopped them into handy pieces. Every piece of soap was shaped differently, as Mama had cut it. She filled bottles with the lye and used it in her washing and for scouring the floor.

Regina didn't want to use Mama's soap to wash herself with anymore and she wrinkled her nose, but when Mama told her that she'd have to buy different soap herself, she gave in. It doesn't matter to me what I wash myself with. But I didn't like the stink it made, and that all our neighbors could smell it, too.

"When the boardinghouse is finished," I said to Mama, "you won't have time to do this anymore. Perhaps you'll even have to hire a washerwoman."

"But, Johnny," said Mama, "that's the time when I'll really need a lot of soap, and it's not so cheap to buy it."

Mama is just accustomed to the old home ways, and won't give them up.

Last week at the Siebenbürgen Society House, we went to hear a sermon by a pastor from our old home. Tata was at work and couldn't come with us. Before we went, we all took baths and put on our best clothes. Everyone would see we were clean folks and also a bit prosperous. Many people were gathered in the Society House; most of them hadn't been in America for very long. I've never heard as much German spoken in America as I heard that evening. Mama knew a lot of people. Emil's baker was there, as well, and said to Mama that she should apprentice him to the bakery business. "People always have to eat. It's a surefire job." Mama was nodding. I don't think Emil will become a baker, though, because he likes to sleep late. Maybe he'll be a night watchman.

Everyone was dressed up for a celebration. There were also some children among the company. Mama had warned us—that is, Emil and me—that we'd have to mind our manners. At that, Regina, who was carrying George in her arms, nodded her head for emphasis. Why does she always have to be so grown-up! I don't know what else we'd have done besides mind our manners. We were sitting on a bench next to one another and Mama had given me the hymn book to hang on to, since she kept having to shake hands.

The pastor began to preach, and it became so still in the hall you could have heard a pin drop: "Time is money. You often hear this in America. It's the first sentence an immigrant in this land learns. But this sentence contains merely part of the truth. It is like a new coat with a big hole in it. Time is surely not money alone. I admit that man makes time into money—in America more so than in other places, and also more than is necessary to live and to buy oneself the good things of life. But doesn't it harm life, if one uses one's lifetime only to make money? Many immigrants have told me that they want to enjoy their lives and freedom here in America. But for many, that doesn't mean anything besides cash and beer. Young people are ensnared by dancing, gambling, and the craving for alcohol . . ."

I scrunched down under the harsh words of the pastor, and had to think about Regina's wild night of dancing. I shot a glance over at her and was amazed that Regina was not at all bowed down to the floor by her guilt; but instead, she was staring the pastor boldly in the face. Afterward, she said to me, "The pastor can't possibly know how wonderful it is to dance the one-step or the Boston." She'd probably been thinking that just as the pastor was scolding about dancing, playing cards, and drinking, and admonishing the young people to think about the future. I thought it was a good thing we weren't Catholic. I knew one Catholic—Martin from Austria. When he'd taken his sister dancing, he had to go to confession and then pray many rosaries. I'd rather confide my secrets to my diary than to the preacher.

While I was lost in my thoughts, I missed a bit of the sermon. A fly had settled on my hand and I was trying to catch it, but it was quicker than I was. Regina was scowling. George wanted to be held by me, but Regina simply put him down on Mama's lap. The fly crawled most disrespectfully off my hand and onto the hymn book and that gave me the idea of opening it. Now it was scrabbling its way over the letters of "A Mighty Fortress Is Our God," and when it reached, "He makes us free of every want," Emil, who had entirely forgotten that we were at a church service, swatted the fly with all his might. Regina took the hymn book away from us and a few people turned and looked at us. Emil and I, however, were sitting looking forward nicely, as though it had been Regina who had slapped at the fly. She'd turned red as a beet.

"Time is certainly not just work and money," the pastor was continuing in his sermon. "You immigrants work a great deal, in order to pay back your debts, to save money so that your wives and children can join you, or so that you may build a house. But you must also have rest and refreshment, or you will break down." Mama was nodding in agreement, as if the pastor were speaking her inmost thoughts.

In the meantime, the fly had moved from me to Emil. Emil shooed it away and it settled on the white collar of a man with a fat red neck who was sitting directly in front of us. I could have smashed it good there, but of course I kept still. The man grabbed at the fly and got it. Emil laughed out loud, although he tried to hold his laughter in, and when I saw him laughing behind his hand, I had to laugh as well. We bent our heads way down as if we had to tie our boot-laces, and didn't look at each other for fear that we'd start laughing again. It was only when I looked into Mama's stern, reproachful face, that I could compose myself enough to once again follow the sermon.

"Many of you are employed in work that no American wants to do," said the pastor, and I had to think about my brother Peter, who had said the same thing. We hadn't heard from him for a long time. Maybe he didn't have the time to write. I always had time to think and to dream. Time wasn't just money, as the pastor was saying. I often spent it on dreams, because they were so lovely. I imagined that one day I'd invent an airship with which you could fly all over, very fast—to California and to Siebenbürgen, to Pittsburgh and to Cleveland—and with this airship I'd travel all over the world. I'd furnish it just like a Pullman car—with salons and sleeping cabins. A few days before, I'd seen just such a railway car in the news-paper. It traveled all across America, from the East Coast to the West Coast, and back again.

"Are you daydreaming again?" Mama was saying and stroking me gently on my head. I pulled my head away; I don't like it when she does that, as if I were a little kid. Emil had fallen asleep leaning against my shoulder.

"Maybe it was too long for the boys," Mama was saying.

"We should have left them at home," Regina agreed with her.

That got me hot under the collar. "That's the last time I'll escort you to your friend Hilde's, if you're going to be so nasty to me." I looked at Regina quite innocently although I was blackmailing her. Embarrassed, she fell silent, and from that moment on, I had a very loving older sister.

We left soon after the sermon, because George was fussing and Mama was tired.

"Do stay a bit longer," said the woman next to us. "We see one another so seldom. The pastor is right; we've got to take more time to talk with one another." Mama was nodding. "Maybe I'll come over to visit. Your niece Emily is going to be a teacher, isn't she?"

"Yes," said our neighbor. "You should talk to her. Perhaps that could be something for Regina as well."

Regina was standing at the door. She'd already laid George in the baby carriage and was beckoning us. "Come on!"

The rest of us were tired and quiet. Only Regina was lively. "Did you see," she said, "how many men there were wearing mustaches?" I hadn't noticed that, but of course she was right again. Regina had apparently been looking at men very carefully for some time now. "So what?" I said. After all, our father had a mustache, too.

"That's how you can tell a foreigner right off. Real Americans are clean-shaven; anyway, those in the city."

My brother Peter had shaved off his mustache as soon as he arrived in America. I checked out the spot on my lip where a mustache would grow, but nothing was there yet. Everything was nice and smooth, and I resolved to be a real American like my brother Peter.

Guests

ama would have liked to have a bench in front of the house, like the one we had in Siebenbürgen. She could sit there in the evening, shelling beans or peas, knitting or mending holes in socks, and having a chat with the neighbor women. But it wasn't the custom here. Youngstown's a city with almost fifty thousand inhabitants, not a village. In America, wives don't sit in front of their houses.

Thank God, Regina says. Those wives, sitting in front of those houses, were nothing but spies. They saw everything; they knew everything; and they passed everything on.

In Youngstown, the men stand around on the street. Mostly they stand in front of the saloon after going to church on Sunday and talk about politics and work. Tata says he doesn't know anything about politics, and most of the immigrants are the same way. They like to talk mostly about news from home. When someone's received a letter, he tells all about what was in it. How the harvest will be (that interests my father); whose hens have the pox and who has died (that interests my mother); who has gotten married (that's exactly what Regina wants to know); and who's gone and immigrated. Emil and I aren't interested in this news at all. Why would I care to know that the cow of my grandparents' neighbor has calved? I'm interested in what's in the newspapers I sell. Whether there's going to be a strike in the steel mill, or whether you can become president of the United States if you go to school in Youngstown!

Emil isn't interested in anything, and George, who is the first real American in our family, is completely occupied with eating, drinking, and making messes in his diapers.

One Sunday evening after grace had been said, and just as Tata had begun telling us the news he'd heard in front of the saloon, someone knocked at our door. We weren't expecting anyone. We broke off our conversation and looked expectantly at the door. "Come in," called Mama and stood up to welcome the guest. The door was opened timidly and a woman holding a girl by the hand stepped into the entrance. You could tell that she'd just arrived from Europe, because nobody in Youngstown walks around in such traditional dress.

"John Smith sent us," the woman was saying. "His boardinghouse is full. And he won't take a woman and child into his house."

Mama looked sharply at the woman and asked her about her background. Her name was Maria Brand; the girl was named Rosina, and they came from a village near Heimburg.

"And who is Rosina's father?" Mama wanted to know.

Maria got very red in the face, and said, with a steady voice, "The farmer I was working for as a housemaid."

"Ah," Mama said, and after a while that seemed like an eternity to me, she added, "well, then, you can't have had an easy time of it." Mama put two more plates on the table and the newcomers sat down and we all ate our evening meal.

"But the boardinghouse isn't even finished," grumbled Regina, who wasn't at all happy about our new guests. After all, our house wasn't very big. "Besides, you said you were going to take in only men."

Mama looked severely at Regina. "I've decided differently, Regina. Before long, when you're back in school, Rosina can help me around the house, and maybe Maria can help with the washing in her spare time."

Mama decided that Mary and Rosie (I called them that; after all, they wanted to be Americans) should sleep on the bed set up in the kitchen. Maybe even in the next few days, Mary could begin work as a washerwoman for a family on our street, while Rosie could stay at home with Mama and Regina and look after George and also help on the farm. Mary and Rosie were very happy with Mama's proposals.

Only Regina was unhappy. When Mary and Rosie had gone to collect their baggage from John Smith's, she said, "You said that men earn more and will pay more."

"Yes," said Mama. "But they also drink more and make more work." In the end, however, it was something else that was the deciding factor for Mama. "Did you see that child?" she asked. "Something about her reminds me of Eliss. I don't know what it is."

"Rosina has brought us the Siebenbürgen summer sky, the pale blue sky, in her eyes," said Father.

So Rosie proved to be lucky for Mary. We liked Rosie right from the start. Things were a little rockier with her mother. Even on the first day, she gave us *trouble.* Mama wanted to bleach the washing and she sent her to the drugstore for some calcium chloride. Mary walked into the first drugstore and asked, "Speak you German?" The druggist answered, "No." *"Dann geben Sie mir für zehn Cents Chlorkalk."* The druggist answered, "I don't understand you."

*"Well, dann don't, du, Döskopp,"** Mary said. She went into four more drugstores, got lost, and was brought back home by the police. Without the bleach.

---

* "Slowpoke."

Rosie learned English faster than her mother. After only a short time, it already seemed to us that she'd always been a part of the family. Mary landed a position as a housemaid for a German family, and in her spare time helped Mama with the washing; Rosie simply stayed with us.

One Sunday afternoon, when our parents had gone to the Society House, Regina decided to make Rosie into a proper American. A real one had to know how to dance.

Together, we shoved the kitchen table to one side so we could have a big dance floor. About her shoulders, Regina draped Mama's carefully guarded lace table-cloth—the one that Grandmother had crocheted and which was only laid on the table on Sundays—and climbed up on a stool. She was the singer on the stage, but also the dance instructor. She was going to direct us from above. Rosie sat on her bed, holding George in her arms and marveling at all the American-ness. Regina hummed a tango melody and made passionate gestures; I was afraid she was going to fall off the stool. She explained to us that in Argentina people danced with great passion. Regina was up on everything. Rosie first had to dance with Emil, but because he couldn't understand how, Regina got down from the stool and danced with Rosie herself. Then Rosie caught on pretty quickly. Emil found it hard, though, and didn't like it. "When you're old enough to go dancing, the tango won't be fashionable anymore," said Regina and let him be.

Then it was my turn. I had to hold Rosie in my arms and look into her eyes, but I couldn't look at her. Rosie was looking up at me with her pale blue eyes, because she was shorter than I was, and all of a sudden I had all the soot and coal dust of Youngstown in my eyes and all the heat of the steel mills in my body.

"Why are you looking past her?" demanded Regina, from her stool. "You can do that with the one-step, maybe, but it won't do for the tango. You have to dance with passion!"

As it ended up, Regina and Rosie danced the dance of passion and I watched them. I resolved to practice the steps on my own, when it was my turn to fetch eggs from the farm, and then, if Rosie should take it into her head to go dancing with Regina, I could go along and dance with her. I didn't like it when Regina was watching me dance. I couldn't concentrate on my feet. I'd already stepped on Rosie's feet a few times, and it didn't seem to bother her. But then Regina had to show her prickly side. "Look out, you oaf! You'll squash her toes."

It was a good thing our parents never stayed long at the Society House, so our dance hour was soon over. We shoved the table back to its place, and Regina folded the wrinkled tablecloth and put it back to its place. Then she laid the table for supper and Rosie helped her. I went out and walked on the street for a bit, to keep an eye out for our parents. Really, though, I wanted to be alone for a while. The heat in my body hadn't subsided. I could feel where my cheek had lightly brushed Rosie's cheek as I bent down to her while we were dancing. I kept thinking about Rosie the whole time, about her eyes and also about her fine hands, and I considered what I could do for Rosie so that later she wouldn't get raw, red hands like her mother had gotten from doing laundry.

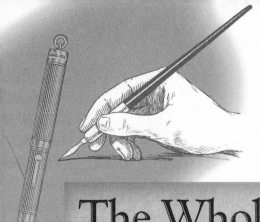

The Whole Family Writes a Letter

Writing letters is hard work for my father. He can lay bricks, work at a blast furnace, and slaughter a pig; when it's necessary, he can repair Mama's handcart and even mend our shoes. But, as a matter of fact, he can't write letters. And Mama doesn't have the time. My parents are very happy whenever a letter arrives from Europe. But once they've read it, they begin groaning, "Now we have to answer the letter." They put it off from week to week until, finally, I write it. Actually, the whole family dictates it and I just write it down. Because this takes so long, I have time to write a bit about me in it as well—the stuff that I think of at that moment. Eventually, the sheet of paper is all covered, and then the letter is finished.

Mama darns socks or mends our pants, and Tata props his head on his hands and says, after he's mulled it over for a while, "Write, Johnny." I then write the beginning of the letter, which is always the same: "Dear Mother, dear Father, dear Brothers and Sisters and In-laws, Nieces and Nephews, and dear Neighbors. Things are well with us and we hope with you, too."

Yesterday, we got a letter from Aunt Kathi and her husband, the ones who made their honeymoon trip to Venice. They want to know exactly what life in America is like, because they're contemplating immigrating. But they haven't reached a final decision and want to wait for our letter, first.

"I don't know what I should advise them to do," said my father, sighing. "If I write that they should come, and then things go badly for them, I'll be at fault."

Mama was dictating: "If things are going badly for you, immigrate. But if things are going well for you, better stay put."

"You've got to understand one thing," Tata was dictating. "Everything's different here. First, you've got to learn English. Even the milk cows here have English names. And there's always something new to learn. Some immigrants count too heavily on their European schooling, but here the children of even the poorest workers can go to school until they're fourteen years old, and they don't have to pay for it. Still, there are a lot of people here who can't read and write at all."

Then Regina was putting a word in: "If you get in
with an American family, you'll learn the language
in a year. Some immigrants, however, don't speak
any English even after five or eight years."

Regina had put away her embroidery, taken an
old, broken-down boot that she had scoured clean,
and placed it on a newspaper she had laid on the
table. She was decorating the boot with a red and
blue bow.

"What on earth are you doing to that boot?" asked
Mama, astonished.

"It's an *antique.* I'm going to hang it on the wall.
It's all the fashion."

"What foolishness," Tata said and smiled.

"You have to follow every fashion, Regina? Every
folly!" Mama said, but she meant no harm.

Regina hung the boot on the wall in our bedroom.
Now we're fashionable and antique at the same time.

After this interruption, I began writing our letter
again. It was Mama's turn: "I go outdoors and look at
the sky, and have no idea which direction the rain is
coming from. I've lost my sense of direction. But
things aren't going badly with us. There's enough to
eat. Everyone can eat butter when they want to. The
rich people, however, only eat until they're half full,
because Americans don't want to get fat. The houses
are bigger than the ones at home, and there are carpets
on the floors, so that you only seldom have to scour
the floor with lye."

George had begun to cry, so Mama put aside the sock she was mending and tended to him. His diapers needed changing. This would go on until he didn't need diapers anymore, and then Mama would have an easier time with him.

Then Tata spoke, "Write what we know about Peter. He's now living in California, only about fifteen kilometers from San Diego. The Colorado River is twice as large as the Danube. It only rains there twice a year and everything has to be irrigated. Water for the irrigation is pumped out of a dam and into canals. The soil is very good, and doesn't need manuring. Barley stalks will yield thirty-five kernels; wheat, forty to fifty kernels. They can be sowed and harvested twice a year. You don't harvest the barley with scythes, like in Siebenbürgen, but with machines. Cotton brings in a lot of money, too, but it takes a lot of work. Melons and grapes yield good harvests. Every farmer lives on his property and the children go to school by buggy, by car, or with the streetcar."

Then my father couldn't think of anything more to say, and I stuck a few sentences of my own into the letter: "George just fell down. He puts everything he finds in his mouth and is always sucking on his dirty thumbs. He's getting his teeth."

I enjoy writing letters, but only when you can do so spontaneously. This one was dragging a bit. It was an important and difficult letter that we were writing.

Tata had opened a bottle of beer and was quenching his thirst. George grabbed for the bottle, and began whining when my father wouldn't give it to him. I drew a moon face in the margin of the letter: dot, dot, comma, slash; the moon face was finished. Next to it, I wrote: "George is howling."

At last, Mama sat down beside me again. "The churches here," Mama was saying, "woo the people. There's a lot of rivalry among them. They're always organizing picnics, and the preacher goes from door to door, fund-raising. By raising funds, the Siebenbürgen Sachsen community bought a church in Youngstown for twelve-thousand dollars. But not everyone here goes to church the way they did in our village. Some have become godless. There are also Siebenbürgen Sachsens who have left the Evangelical church and gone over to the Baptists or the Adventists."

All this writing had left us hungry, and Mama began preparing supper for us. Regina was helping her. Recently, Regina has been very cheerful, because she's going back to school this fall. She sings again, and Tata has been giving her violin lessons every Sunday afternoon, since a teacher should have command of a musical instrument.

Tata praised me for my good handwriting and started dictating again: "You've got to stay on your guard against the swindlers among our own countrymen, if you come here. They'll talk to you in our mother tongue, offer their services to you, and at the end, all your money will have disappeared."

"You absolutely have to write down," Mama was saying, "that Americans often seek divorces, and that there are men here who have two wives; one in

Europe nobody knows about, and one here. That's called bigamy and is forbidden by law."

It occurred to Regina that we hadn't written anything about Thanksgiving. I wrote: "On the fourth Thursday in November, everybody has a *dinner* and there's a turkey on every table, and an English plum pudding. Afterward, everyone says thank you, because it tasted good to them."

Then the letter was finally finished, and Mama was saying I should end up with nice greetings to everybody. I wrote down the sentence we ended all our letters with: "We send you our heartfelt greetings from faraway," and then all our names underneath.

After supper, Tata decided to go to the boardinghouse again, to do a bit more tidying up of the construction site. Just on the point of leaving, he stopped and said, very thoughtfully, "Mariekins, did we praise America too much? When they read our letter, they'll think that Paradise is here in America."

"I have no idea where Paradise is," said Mama. "Maybe it's enough to hope for it."

Then while Mama and Regina washed the dishes, I put George to bed and read Emil a story before he went to sleep. Rosie sat with us and listened. "No one's ever read a story to me before," she said. I would have liked to go on reading and reading, but Mama said, "Don't you see that Emil's been asleep for a long time already?" So I stopped reading, and retreated to my diary. Maybe someday, I'll read some of it out for Rosie: about how we immigrated. Maybe she'd like to know.

The Long Road to America

An Afterword

About one hundred years ago, over five million immigrants from Eastern and Southeastern Europe crossed present-day Germany in order to board ships from the German harbors—especially those of Bremerhaven and Hamburg. This migration of people was scarcely noticed by the German populace, since most of the transients arrived directly at the harbors in immigrant trains or other special trains. It had been feared that some of these people would stay behind in the German Empire and become a burden to the state. Hence, the German Empire's interest in a controlled and speedy transit.

There had already been one great wave of immigration to America around the time of the

Revolution of 1848. Dutch, Flemish, English, Prussian, Sachsen, Thüringen, Irish, Scandinavian, and French people had immigrated. The German shipping lines (the Hamburg-America and the North German-Lloyd line in Bremen) had carried a great portion of the transoceanic passengers. When this great wave of immigration ebbed, the shipping lines began to turn their attention to Eastern Europe, and thousands of shipping agents went to Austria-Hungary, Russia, Serbia, and Rumania to facilitate passage to the German ports for those wishing to immigrate.

The reasons for this great migration to America may be traced back to a multitude of factors. Many people (for instance, the impoverished farmers of Austria-Hungary, and the persecuted Jews of Russia and Rumania) were hoping for a better life in America, where industry was rapidly evolving and labor was sought. Improvements in rail and steamship transportation, however, first made this mass migration possible.

Usually, one member of a family—the husband or a grown son—would set out on the great journey and the rest of the family (often traveling on prepaid tickets) would follow after. The steamship agents lent the travelers practical assistance, for which they were well paid. There were also smugglers who would take people without passports over the border. Using propaganda songs printed on peddled leaflets, the agents recruited people for the immigration.

Other propaganda songs were written opposing the immigration. These, too, were brought to the attention of the public by leafleting. Their aim was to persuade useful workers and taxpayers to stay at home in their native lands.

The journey of the immigrants was long and difficult. The immigrants traveled by train through many lands and across many borders. They made an uncomfortable crossing by ship, and then often had to travel further by train to the coal and steel regions in western Pennsylvania and eastern Ohio, or to West Virginia, northern Illinois, or Indiana. Not everyone who undertook the rigors of the journey was permitted entry to America, however.

On arrival in America, many people were turned away and sent back to their homelands at the expense of the shipping lines. Some of these people were sick, some were handicapped, and some were poor people with many small children who would be likely to become a burden on the public welfare. As the number of people sent back rose, the shipping lines began to establish inspection stations at the borders. Anyone unlikely to succeed in meeting the American immigration criteria was turned back at these stations. Only the steerage passengers, who comprised the greater part of the immigrants, had to pass these inspections. The well-to-do cabin passengers were inspected neither at the German border nor upon arrival in America, since it was felt that they had enough means at their disposal to manage without governmental help.

The immigration of this great population came to a halt in August 1914, at the beginning of the First World War, when the English blockaded German borders.

In New York harbor, these migrants became immigrants. In America they were greeted with mixed feelings. A great number of Americans of Anglo-Saxon descent feared that the new immigration would bring foreign domination of the country. The tenement slums, the newcomers' ethnic insularity, a perception that they lacked education and literacy, their alleged predisposition toward criminal behavior, and competition in the labor market all combined to foster fears among many Americans that the new immigrants could not adapt to American values and standards of living. These Americans demanded stricter controls on immigration.

There were also, however, those who supported immigration. They spoke out for the tradition of the "open door" and fought to integrate the newcomers into American society by means of language programs and reeducation measures.

Now, one hundred years have passed, and those immigrants from Eastern and Southeastern Europe, their children, grandchildren, and great-grandchildren have long been Americans.

My book is based upon immigrants' letters from 1902 to 1986. For them, I owe a debt of thanks to the

Sill family, formerly from Youngstown, and their descendents in America, Canada, and Germany.

A special thanks is also owed Rohtraut and Joachim Wittstock in Rumania, who placed the writings of their teacher and pastor grandfather, Oskar Wittstock, at my disposal. Wittstock undertook a journey to America in 1908 and reported in great detail about the living conditions of German immigrants who had come from Siebenbürgen.

Thanks, too, to all those whose research on immigration helped me acquire the knowledge necessary to write this book.

—Karin Gündisch

4/3   11/02   5-31-03